PUPPY LOVE

Summer of Adventures 5

Alex Silver

CONTENTS

COPYRIGHT

SYNOPSIS

Impulse control is not my darling puppy's strong suit. Most of the time, I find that endearing. It certainly helps us find willing partners to join us for a scene or two. As long as it doesn't put Quent in a position to get hurt, I'm on board. But when their spontaneity combined with their huge heart results in them offering to be their brother's surrogate, let's just say, I have my doubts.

Quent refuses to be deterred from their path despite the risks. As their mommy, my number one job is to take care of them, no matter my misgivings. That includes arranging the details and supporting them through the pregnancy and beyond. If we're both lucky, I might just get to give them every kinky desire of their heart along the way.

Quent and I have learned over the years that we can resolve most of our problems with clear communication, I just hope that includes the bumps along the way to helping my brothers-in-law grow their family.

Puppy Love is an F/X puppy play love story between an established couple. Kylee is a transgender web designer and Mommy to Quent, a nonbinary pharmacy technician and pup. It includes puppy play, surrogacy, pregnancy (and related gender dysphoria and anxiety around medical care), ethical non-monogamy, light medical/veterinary kink, breeding kink, and boot worship.

CHAPTER 1

Quent

"Hey, Quent," Jared calls me as I'm leaving the pharmacy at the end of my shift. Weird, since he knows I'm headed to his place to watch my nephew so he and his husband, Logan, can have a date night tonight. His voice sounds off, hoarse. Like he's sick or upset. I pause in the pharmacy parking lot in case he needs me to bring him some cold meds or something.

"Hi, is everything alright?" I ask.

"Not really," Jared chokes out the words, and my stomach drops.

"Did something happen to Thomas?" I ask, heart in my throat.

"He's fine. Everyone is safe, but he's with his mom." And then my brother spills the entire story and my confusion turns to heartbreak. For my brother and for the fact Thomas won't be a part of my life anymore. This must have left Jared and Logan both devastated. I've heard my brother's voice hoarse from tears before. The entire adoption process has been a rocky road for them.

Jared has always been my rock, and this is the most heartbroken I've ever heard him. He sounds wrecked, and he has to pause to collect himself between words. For now, I'm just numb. The news isn't quite real to me yet. I don't want it to sink in that I don't have a nephew anymore. That my brother had to say goodbye to the baby who was supposed to be his son.

When Jared called to tell me he and Logan got matched with a newborn after years of exhausting every adoption option at their disposal, I was speechless. And anyone who knows me knows how rare that is. I pretty much left work mid-shift and hopped in my car to get my new little nibling a 'welcome to the family' gift. Slight exaggeration, I took an early lunch to go shopping, but still, it was the best news. I'm lucky the pharmacists who own the place are supportive as well as queer friendly.

The entire process happened faster than any of us expected. In a matter of weeks, Jared and Logan were meeting their little holiday miracle and bringing him home. Thomas's birth mom only found out she was pregnant when she was already over two-thirds of the way through her pregnancy. That limited her options when she chose Jared and Logan to raise her baby.

Thomas was everything they'd dreamed of when they decided to start a family several years and thousands of dollars in various fees and courses and baby gear later. And then their entire world fell apart this morning, when Thomas's birth mother changed her mind about being able to raise him. It's not the first time an adoption fell through for them, but it's the first time it happened after they had a child in their arms. Living in their home for the past few weeks.

A social worker came to collect Thomas from them this morning. Jared waited until I got out of work to call me with the news. As soon as we're off the phone, I start my car to rush over to console him. When I arrive at his and Logan's place, they're in the living room, huddled together on their couch. The baby gear that littered this room the last time I visited appears to have been hastily shoved into the closet. A pastel green pacifier trails on the floor where the leg of the baby swing has left the closet door wedged open a crack.

That's when it really hits me that the sweet little baby I've held on their couch and fed a bottle to isn't here anymore. He'll never be here again. He's safe, and healthy and loved, and he's gone just as surely as if he'd never been at all. Just like Mom and Dad. Gone forever. For now, I shove down the grief. I can't break when Jared and Logan need me.

I wish I could have been here to tidy away anything that might remind them of their loss. That stupid pacifier shouldn't be here, salt in a raw wound. I'm struck with the visceral urge to kick that sad little reminder of everything they've lost deep into the closet. Shove the door closed and lock it all away where it can't hurt. Make it all go away. Make it not hurt. And I can't.

All I can do is to be here for them, so I take a deep breath and focus on my brother. Jared is even more of a wreck than he sounded on the phone. I've never seen him so grief-stricken. Not even when we lost our parents in a car accident after my high school graduation. Or when he had to take guardianship of me in the aftermath and deal with my seventeen-year-old angst over the whole situation.

Jared hadn't even been this upset when the stress of working out how to finance their adoption almost ended in a divorce. He went so far as to stay in our guest room for a few days. That was before he and Logan decided to foster instead of pursuing another private adoption. And after their first several attempts at using an international agency fell through for various reasons. As far as I know, he hadn't even grieved like this when their last match for a newborn ended in a miscarriage. Today, I'm watching my brother face utter devastation. It's hard to see that he isn't unbreakable. It hurts.

I want to rage at anything that could cause him this much pain, but I can't really be mad that Thomas got reunited with his birth family. Just sad that he isn't Jared's to keep after he and Logan have already gone through this before. And I don't think either of them has it in them to go through the uncertainty of whether they'll get to keep their baby again. It's awful to sit there while my big brother, a fount of stability in my life, sobs on Logan's shoulder.

I've seen him cry before, but I've never seen him give up and it's scary. The same sort of squirming dread in my guts I got when I didn't know where I'd end up after they told us Mom and Dad were dead. Like I'm untethered from reality and everything I thought I knew is changing before my eyes.

It leaves me desperate to offer him some shred of hope. I fidget with the futile need to do something, anything, to make the unfixable better. Jared has been there to pick up my pieces in the past, when I felt broken after our parents died. I want nothing more than to repay him, at least a portion of what he's done for me. The sacrifices he made to make sure I'd be okay. I grasp for any potential lifeline out of his grief.

"Is there a plan to try again? Surrogacy? Or another adoption?" I ask, hoping to divert his attention toward planning the future. That's something Jared is good at. Logan meets my eyes with a bleak expression and gives a subtle shake of his head, warning me off. But the question is already out there, hanging over us.

Silence stretches, Jared clings to his husband and I realize that I maybe shouldn't be here. That they need time alone to grieve and I can only offer to bring them dinner or be there when they are ready to face the world again. That prickling sense of discomfort, the bone-deep realization that I'm intruding on something intensely private, grows the longer I sit there, making me antsy and restless.

I should get up and leave, except an abrupt departure would be even worse at this point. No way out but through. I really need to think before I act. It's something Mommy tells me all the time, and I try, but my brother needed me, so there's nowhere else I could be tonight.

"One of us could miraculously grow a womb," Logan quips with a snort of near-hysterical laughter that says he is trying to hide how deeply he is hurting.

"No." Jared pulls out of his husband's arms and shakes his head, trying to pull himself together for me. "I think that's it. I can't live with worrying that someone is going to change their mind and crush our dreams again." Jared rubs at his eyes and Logan takes his hand. "I just don't have that in me." The two of them share volumes as their eyes meet. It's the sort of look I exchange with Mommy sometimes. When there aren't words for something too big to handle on my own. An understanding that's just between us.

"What if it was someone you trusted already who offered to be the surrogate?" The half-baked start of a plan is coming together in my head. I block out the internal alarm bells that this might be a terrible idea. My pulse quickens with a combination of nerves at what I'm about to do and the thrill of maybe being able to help after all. My heart pounds loud enough to drown out the little voice of dysphoria in my head that is *horrified* at what I'm saying, but I have to say it. I don't have to be helpless in the face of their grief, even if what I'm considering scares me.

"Like who? It's not as though we never considered that route, but it's not like we can just pay someone to give us a baby, Q. You might be able to pay for a surrogate in the States, but in Canada, the gestational carrier has to do it out of the goodness of their heart. And it's a lot to ask of someone."

"Didn't your cousin offer a few years ago?" I ask Logan, hoping for one last out.

"Yeah. She said if we were still trying once her family was complete that she would consider it. But that was before she almost hemorrhaged while giving birth to her daughter. Afterward, she found out she has a clotting disorder that makes it risky for her to carry another child. I wouldn't ask her to take that risk. We might just have to rethink what parenthood might look like. There are loads of older kids who need a home, even if it's not permanent."

"Yeah. That's a good idea." I nod. If it hadn't been for Jared taking me in, there were six months where I'd have been one of those kids. Another teen who needed a place to land between my parents dying and my eighteenth birthday. And if I'm honest, well beyond that arbitrary cutoff. He helped me figure out how to be an adult.

I know first-hand that they'd be good at providing a loving home for teens. But I also know they want to experience the baby years too. And I have the power to give them that. So, I make the offer before I can chicken out, knowing that Jared would never ask this of me only makes my need to step up for him more intense. "You should totally do that too. But if you still want a baby, I can do it. And then the baby could even share genes with both of you."

Jared stares at me for a long moment, hope warring with concern in his eyes. He knows just how big an offer this is for me. He's the one who held me when I cried over the way my body developed as a teen. I shared my real name with him before I told anyone else. Jared was the first to call me Quent. The first person to use my correct pronouns. The one who helped me change my gender marker and name on all my legal documents. He helped me stick with it until I found a doctor willing to help me transition without pushing me to be someone I'm not.

My brother gave me everything I needed when I needed him without a word of complaint. He was putting himself through law school and he'd just lost his parents too, but he was the guardian I needed, despite all of that. And now that he needs me, there is no way I can do anything less for him. I'm as certain of that as I've ever been about anything.

I'm also terrified of what it will mean, but that's something I can deal with later. For now, I ruthlessly crush the emotions down, along with my personal grief over Thomas. Something to deal with when I'm home and safe with Mommy.

I focus on my brother. He's still plastered against his husband, but he's not crying for the moment. He's gazing into me with those laser-eyes of parental assessment, as though he can read my very soul. Jared knows exactly how much I'm offering him. He took me to a counselor to deal with all the garbage in my head about what I should be versus who I was on the inside. Not to mention handling that on top of my grief. Jared knows me and he knows how hard this will be for me better than almost anyone.

"You don't owe us that, Q." Jared means it, but I can hear the ache of longing, the barest thread of hope underlying his words.

I shake my head, denying that I'm offering out of obligation. "Duh, I know. I *want* to give you this, Jar. You've always been the best big brother a person could ask for. You and Logan are amazing dads. I want to give you the chance to try. If I can. I mean, I don't see why I couldn't. But I'll make an appointment with whichever doctor I need to see to find out if we can make this happen. And I'll sign whatever papers you need to be sure the kid belongs to you and Logan, okay?"

"You should take some time to think about it, Quent. You're sweet to offer, but I don't want to get my hopes up again. Not if you've got any doubts." Jared dashes tears away from his eyes.

"Yeah, I get that. I'll make the appointments and let you know, okay?" I insist.

"Alright. Thanks." Jared sniffles.

After that, I offer to pick up takeout for them, and then I head for home. It's only as I'm pulling into my driveway behind Mommy's bicycle that I realize I've fucked up colossally. Like, the kind of mistake that could destroy everything that matters in my life. I didn't mean to do it. Somehow I doubt that telling the love of my life it was an accident that I offered my brother my womb is going to make this better. I should have asked Mommy about this first.

I should talk to her now. Right now. I should tell her what I did. Instead, I text my best friend.

Quent: Can you talk?

I shift around in the driver's seat, propping my phone against the steering wheel. Did Mommy hear me pull into the driveway? If she did, I might not have long before she comes out to see why I'm lurking in the car instead of coming inside. Or why I'm home so early when I was supposed to be babysitting. The reminder is like a gut-punch. I'm not ready to face my grief about Thomas yet. I bite my fist and shove it back down. Luckily, Connor gets back to me fast.

Connor: Sure. What's up?

Quent: So, I think I made a stupid.

Connor: You think, or you know?

Quent: *dramatic sigh* I know I fucked up royally and I'm scared to tell Mommy.

I squirm in my seat, eager to vent to Connor. He doesn't have a stake in this, so it's easier to say it to him first. And the longer I draw this confession out, the longer I can put off admitting what I've all but promised already. I finger my collar, the reminder that I belong to Mommy. That she gets a say in what I do with my life and my body, and I just bulldozed over that agreement. What if she considers this a breach of trust? I can't lose her any more than I could sit by and watch Jared suffer.

Connor: Whatever it is, you can't undo it, right? She's going to find out and it will go better if you're honest with her.

Quent: Poo. You're not letting me wallow.

I stick my tongue out at the phone, even though Connor can't see the gesture.

Connor: You can come over to my place to whine about how unfair it is that you have to deal with the consequences of your actions. After you tell your Mommy what rule you broke.

That's tempting, despite his room being little more than a partitioned off alcove in his apartment's living room. I wish he was holding me right now, comforting me and helping me find the wherewithal to go inside and tell Mommy what I did. I wish she was holding me and telling me I didn't mess up too badly for us to fix it.

Quent: It wasn't a rule.

Quent: This time.

Quent: It was worse than that.

Connor: Vague much?

I can picture him rolling his eyes at me. I shift in my seat, glancing up at the door to see if Mommy is coming to check on me. She's not in the doorway, so she probably didn't notice my arrival yet.

Quent: I made an offer to Jared without thinking it through.

Connor: That doesn't sound so terrible, Q.

Quent: Yeah, that was what I thought when I was making the offer. But it's sort of a big thing. I probably should have asked permission first. Ya know? Since obviously Mommy didn't give me rules for something she'd never have expected me to be impulsive enough to just throw out there on a whim.

Connor: Miss Kylee always says she loves what a generous heart you have. Doing a favor for your brother is exactly what she'd expect you to do, if it's something in your power to offer.

Quent: *groan* Yeah. Except I'm afraid she's going to hate me for this. Especially since it will affect her too.

Connor: I can't imagine Kylee ever hating you, Q.

It helps for him to say what I already know deep down. Mommy and I are solid. We'll get through this. I just don't know quite how yet. I hate the idea of disappointing her. Whatever else she thinks, I know the fact that I offered already, on an impulse without a thought to her stance on the matter, will disappoint her.

Quent: Ugh. I can't imagine it either; I can't lose her. But I don't know if I can take this back. Jared is my brother and there isn't really anyone else he can ask.

Connor: I might have better advice if I had a clue what you are babbling about, Q. Did you offer to give him a kidney?

Quent: Close. It involves the use of my internal organs, anyway. *nervous laugh*

I readjust to prop my phone on my knees and press the heels of my hands over my eyes. I'm not doing a good job explaining. The steering column is in the way, so I can't curl up anymore than this, despite the urge to hug myself tight. I wait for Connor to reply. His response takes a while. When it comes, he's at least appropriately sympathetic.

Connor: Fuck. You should probably talk to your Mommy about that, babe. For what it's worth, if you're not saying what I think you're not saying, that is a very generous offer that you made. I'm sure your brother would appreciate that it's a big deal, and it's something you need to discuss with your partner before you can commit to that.

Quent: You didn't see their faces. He and Logan have been trying to adopt for years.

Connor: Wait. Didn't your brother and his husband just adopt a baby?

Quent: Almost. It fell through at the last minute. That's why I said what I said. And it's why I can't pull the rug out from under them again after putting it out there. I have to at least try.

Connor: Wow. I'm sorry about Thomas. I know you were already pretty attached to the little goober.

That hurts. I have to close my eyes and breathe through the sting of hot tears that I'm not ready to cry over the baby. He isn't ours to love anymore. I want the numbness of not quite believing it back.

Quent: Yeah. I mean, I know it's a good thing that he is going to be with people who love him. I'll miss him. Mostly, I'm sad for Jar and Logan. They're devastated about it, you know? I just needed to do something to give them some hope.

I wish logic made the loss hurt less. For me and for my brother. I'm not going there yet. I need to talk to Mommy before I let myself cry over Thomas.

Connor: I can see that. Your heart was in the right place. Real talk: do you think you can actually go through with carrying a pregnancy? I don't think I could handle that and then give up the kid at the end.

I'm glad Connor changed the subject. Answering his questions makes it easier not to think about being sad. And it helps me to process my jumbled up feelings about surrogacy.

Quent: You mean like mental health/dysphoria-wise? I think it'll be okay? It's kind of a thing I've wanted to do. Except I really don't want a kid to raise. I don't mind sharing my Mommy for a playdate, but I don't think I'd like having her divided attention as a 24/7 thing ;P. Plus, the kid will be my nibling. So I'll get to have fun playtime as their cool relative Q. And then send them home to their dads when they're too sugared up to sleep. Best of all worlds.

Connor: That's good then. If you ever need someone to bitch to about how miserable it all makes you, I can be your guy. My sibs can't seem to stop growing their goblin hordes of grandchildren for mom, so I've heard it all.

Quent: Thanks. I might take you up on that. Kylee doesn't want kids either, but sometimes she's sad it wasn't really a choice in the first place? I mean, barring organ transplants being widely available. Ugh. Sometimes it sucks that we basically get dysphoric about opposite crap, you know?

Connor: I'll bet. But it's nice that you can at least empathize with each other.

Quent: Yep. Wouldn't trade her for anything. Ugh. I need to go talk to her about this, I guess.

That feels right. My fidgety feet want to run to her. I don't think I can manage that right now. Still, the urge to just see her is strong. I need her to smile at me, hold me and tell me everything's alright between us. That it always will be, and nothing I do can tear us apart for long. I need her to envelop me in her maternal warmth.

Connor: You've got this. She won't be mad. At worst, you'll get a punishment for not discussing something so huge with her first, because she still thinks you are capable of learning lessons. :P

Connor unknowingly echoes my thoughts. It will be okay.

Quent: :P Hey! I resemble that remark. Thanks, Con. <3

Connor: Anytime, babe. Now, go find your Mommy and tell her what you did with your big generous heart. Her reaction can't be any worse than whatever wild scenarios you're dreaming up in your head. And call me to let me know how it all goes, okay?

Quent: I will. Thanks for the pep talk. Wish me luck?

I gather up my work stuff, making sure not to forget anything I might need in the car, and swing open the door. The car beeps at me, reminding me to turn off the lights.

Connor: Luck.

I take my time getting out of the car. Connor helped me process everything. And I'm not as anxious about the coming conversation as I was before we talked. I still don't want to tell Mommy everything that happened today, but she'll take one look at me and know I need to spill my guts.

Telling her will make it real. Her soft touches and sympathy will make it impossible to shove down my grief and fear. I'll fall apart when she holds me against her soft curves, curtaining us behind the silky fall of her long hair. She always makes me embrace my emotions in a way no one else can. I don't want to face that it's real.

Thomas is really gone, and I really offered to be a surrogate. To let a baby completely rearrange my internal organs and wreak havoc on my sense of self. I let my hands flutter over my flat chest and belly. A body that comes as close to expressing my internal self as possible when the world insists on making everything binary. A body that will change and betray me if I go through with this. It's a lot and I can't handle it on my own.

I stand in the driveway as I pocket my keys and phone. Before trudging to the door, I double check that I've locked up the car, buying every second I can between now and when I have to let it out.

I hate disappointing Mommy and I have no illusions that she'll be happy about this. As soon as I enter the house, she's going to take one look at me with her piercing brown eyes and know I'm guilty about something. In the end, I know better than to try putting it off any longer, so I take a deep breath, gird up my loins, and walk inside.

CHAPTER 2

Kylee

Q uent sent me a message earlier this evening to remind me they're going to their brother's place after work tonight. I expect them to be late, since they've been enjoying having a nibling to spoil for the past few weeks. I've even got a movie I know they won't like in mind to pass the time until they're home.

First, I need to address some client notes on my latest project. Working from home as a freelance web designer gives my schedule flexibility. It also means I always have to be on top of generating new projects and gaining new clients. It took years to build enough of a portfolio to make a go of running a small business, but I'm glad I took the leap.

While most of my projects fall into run-of-the-mill commercial sites that form my bread and butter, some of them pose fun new challenges that keep work fresh and engaging. Some projects I take aren't about paying the bills. Things like maintaining an indie film fan forum, I do because it's a passion; though now that the site is up and running, it doesn't require much maintenance. So I can just enjoy it as a regular around the forums.

And trading services with my friends in the kink community is a way of building connections. Jax's photography website and Martin's site for Adventures, our kink club, I do because of my relationships with people. Today, my schedule is all about the business side of things though. If I finish the site upgrade I'm working on before Q gets home, I'll be free to take them down to their kennel to burn some energy before bed. Without work hanging over my head, so we can both relax.

The front door easing shut around suppertime breaks my focus. The effort of being quiet isn't like my pup at all. They normally come home from these visits all bouncy and bubbling with excitement. Q loves to play, whether it's with kids, littles, or other pups, they thrive on getting to let out their puppy side. I expected them home buzzing with the sort of energy where they shut the front door a little too hard and the loud thumps of them kicking off their shoes shortly follows.

I've been looking forward to watching my pup frolic and play without a care in the world tonight. Except Quent is home hours before they ought to be if they were hanging out with the baby and that has my Mommy senses at high alert. They aren't acting like themself.

I save out of my project, hibernate the computer and pad into the hallway to check on Quent, expecting them to come bowling into me for a hug any second. They don't. Instead, I make it all the way to the mudroom where they sit plopped on their butt, meticulously trying to unpick the knots from their shoelaces. They barely made it inside far enough to shut the door behind them. Considering that they only ever untie their shoes as an avoidance tactic, I take it as further confirmation something is bothering them.

"There you are. I thought I heard the door." I announce my presence and Quent hunches their shoulders like they want to hide from me. And that seals it. There is definitely something fishy going on here. I am going to find out what it is or at least be certain Quent is alright before the end of the night.

"Hi, Mommy. I got home early." They raise one hand to fiddle with the heart-shaped metal link on their collar. Like they need a reminder that they belong to me before returning to their tangled shoelaces. My chest squeezes tight at the habitual gesture. I love that when they need comfort, it's the tangible reminder of our bond that they seek. At the same time, seeing them so upset and withdrawn makes me ache to fix whatever is wrong.

"I can see that. Didn't you have fun with Thomas?" I press. This is one of those times they need me to be their stern Mommy and not settle for evasions. I crouch down in front of them to get on their level.

"No. They ended up having to give him back."

"What do you mean?" Quent isn't making any sense. It's not like you can just return a baby.

Quent gives up on the shoes and hugs their middle, arms crossed low over their belly as they hunch forward. I want to scoop them up and pepper their cheeks with kisses until that dejected expression is nothing but a memory. But then we won't talk and I need to understand what's going on with my pup.

"His mom changed her mind. So, he's back with her now. Jared and Logan aren't adopting him."

"Ah. I'm so sorry, love. I know how much you loved him already." I can't hold back from touching them at that news, so I pat their ankle.

Quent sniffles and rocks over their folded arms, face a portrait in misery and shame. "I do, but we knew this was a possibility. It's ultimately a good thing for Thomas, even if it sucks for Jared and Logan." They say the words with a complete lack of conviction, reciting a truism. "But that's not all."

"What else happened, pup?" I give them my best stern voice. Much as I want to be soft and comfort them over their loss, I can tell from the quaver in Q's tone that they're on the brink of falling apart. They need me to make them tell me whatever else is bothering them before it can fester. I've known my pup for long enough to read them like a book in most circumstances and they are hurting, but they're also feeling guilty. Like they don't think they deserve the comfort they so obviously need from me.

Quent is still rocking and they won't meet my eyes. That breaks my heart even as it firms my resolve. We need to lance this pain. They have to be hurting more than they're even letting on if they won't look at me. I long to swoop in and scoop them into a hug, but as much as that would make me feel better, I don't think it's what they need. Not yet. "You can tell me anything, love."

"I know. But I'm scared, Mommy." They go back to picking at the knots in their laces.

I step closer and crouch in front of them to help. I make quick work of the knots, easing their feet from their sneakers and pressing a chaste kiss to each of their arches before setting their feet on the ground. Without turning away from them, I reach over to place the shoes in their spot on the rack beside the door. "Nothing you can say will make me stop loving you, Quent."

"Promise you won't be mad?" Their worried gaze darts up to me, their big blue eyes, watery with unshed tears, lock onto mine, needing reassurance. I cup their cheek in my palm, brushing back a few stray strands of their shaggy bleach blonde bob. Their sorrow makes my heart ache for them.

"I promise we'll work through whatever you have to tell me."

"Yeah. About that. I offered to carry a baby for them." Quent admits, wincing.

"Oh." That knocks the wind out of my sails. This isn't something I expected to have to deal with. I thought I knew my pup's limits, and I'd have said this fell well beyond those limits.

"I know I should have discussed it with you before suggesting something so huge, but they were heartbroken. It's the only way

I could think to help make it better."

"You aren't responsible for making this better, Q." I try to keep my voice gentle, but my emotions must come through. A tremor in my voice, and a tenseness in my shoulders as my spine stiffens.

I'm not mad. Not exactly. More, I'm worried about all the parts of this that Quent might not have thought through. Knowing my pup, they've barely thought of anything beyond the fact that they have the means to give someone they love something he desperately wants.

Quent curls up tighter. "Does that mean you don't want me to do it?"

"It means I don't want you to dive in over your head, puppy." I open my arms to them.

Q lunges at me, their weight slamming into me for a tight hug. I catch them with a stifled oomph, bracing against the wall until I catch my balance. Good thing our mudroom is narrow enough that it's easy to catch myself before we both go sprawling. I hold them tight. "Surrogacy will mean a lot of medical appointments, and not the fun kind. It will mean your body changing in ways you won't like. I think it might be hard for both of us, mentally and emotionally. Not to mention the physical parts."

"I fucked up." Quent mumbles into my neck.

"No. You didn't fuck up, Q. It will also mean giving people you love a precious gift that only you can give them. I am proud of you for wanting to do that." I caress behind their ears and they nuzzle into me.

"But?"

"I wish we'd discussed it and figured out a plan together before you put that out there, but what's done is done. You already made the offer, so there is no harm in taking the time to be sure it's a good choice for you. Sleep on it, and in the morning, if you still think it's something you want to do, then we will look at the details together this weekend. But there is one thing I need you to understand. Are you listening, pup?" I take their face between my hands, to be sure they are taking me seriously. Sometimes, when they get overwhelmed by a problem, they retreat into their pupspace. Where they can take comfort in the sound of my voice, with zero heed paid to the meaning of my words.

"Yes, Mommy. I'm listening."

"I need you to promise that if it's too much, and you realize you can't do it, then you back out. No matter what point we're at in the process. If it's too much for you, I don't want you to go through with it. And if you can't promise me that, then I don't know if I can be a party to it." It kills me to give them any kind of ultimatum. I hate having to deny them anything. Setting rules that upset Q is one of the hardest parts of being their Mommy.

The fact this is something so intrinsically tied to their gender identity and bodily autonomy makes it worse. But that's why I have to set this boundary now. My number one job as Q's Mommy is taking care of them. Sometimes that means protecting my puppy when they aren't in an emotional place to protect themself.

I can't sit by while they do something self-destructive, so this is the time to make my boundaries clear, no matter how much it might hurt us both. I have to do it, but it still hurts when their body tenses against me at my words. As though I've just confirmed all their worst fears about having this conversation.

"You'd leave me?" Quent's big expressive eyes brim with more tears as they ask it, and my resolve crumbles at hearing they could think I'd ever turn my back on them.

"No. That's not what I said or what I meant. This is ultimately your decision to make. I promised to be by your side through thick and thin, and I meant it." To emphasize my words, I tug on the heart ring in their collar, the symbol of our commitment to each other. "I'll be here for you no matter what you decide. But I can't endorse a decision that hurts you, Quentin." It's a distinction with little practical difference, but it's one I have to make as clear to them as possible. They have to know there is an exit strategy that I will support no matter what, if they need it.

Quent shivers in my arms. "I don't want to do it without you."

"You won't have to."

"I'm scared."

"I know."

"But I think I want to try, anyway."

"Okay. What do you need from me?"

"Can you help me figure out the logistics? Making the appointments and figuring out the paperwork and if we need to get one of those IVF places involved or if we can just DIY this shit?"

"Of course."

"And um... I kind of want to do it the old-fashioned way."

That throws me for a loop. "Um, can you explain? Because it sounds like you want to fuck your brother-in-law, and that doesn't fall in the scope of what we agreed to."

Quent's libido is pretty much at the opposite end of the frequency spectrum from mine. I'm happy with sex a couple times a month, if that, and they prefer at least a few times a week. Our longstanding solution to that mismatch has been ethical non-monogamy.

For us, that means Quent gets off with their friends when they are in their pupspace. They love to give head and get fucked. I enjoy watching them play with other people, whether or not it's sexual, and they get their needs met. But one of our rules is that they don't engage in fluid exchanges with other people and another is that we keep the drama to a minimum.

Our friends all know that with Q, a blow job is just a blow job. At the end of the day, they are going to be coming home with me. I doubt Jar and Logan have a similar relationship and broaching the subject with them strikes me as all kinds of complicated.

Quent brays with laughter. It's a relief to see some of their spark after the somber mood they came home in. When they pull out of my embrace, I let them go and we sit together on the floor while they bust a gut laughing.

"OMG, no!" They finally find their words. "Just fuck no. Even if he and Jar were into ENM, which, there's no way in hell I'd ever ask them that, I can't imagine getting dicked by Logan. He's practically my brother. Ew." Quent shudders theatrically, then shakes off the very idea. The gesture is definitely a pup move and I can see them slipping toward that headspace. Where they don't need to make the decisions. I was right that they'd need pup time tonight, even if I'd been wrong about the reasons. Still, I want an answer to my question.

"So, it's not about Logan, but you want to be inseminated outside a medical setting?"

Quent nods eagerly. "I want you to breed me. Like, roleplay with you paying for a stud to breed your bitch in heat. Making me give you a litter of pups to give away to good homes."

I blink at them for a second and then ruffle their hair. "That's an old fantasy; you still want it?"

"Yeah. You told me breeding was a limit. And when we talked about if that had changed last year when we were discussing birthday gifts, you didn't seem into it." Quent shrugs, like it's no big deal. But I know what my pup looks like when they're really into something and this is a fantasy they've nurtured for a long time. It matters to them. When they first brought it up, I'd been early in my transition and the idea of breeding them had gotten too tangled up in my personal triggers and dysphoria.

Quent never pushed me for it. Tops have limits, too, and that was one of mine when we started to date. Q can be impulsive as hell, but they respect boundaries. It's weird to realize that particular kink has gone from a hard limit to something I'd consider for them.

Circumstances change, and in the years since they first asked about trying a breeding scene, I've had several procedures that help me feel secure in my body and my identity. And we've built up the kind of trust that I think will be enough to get us through a scene like this. Especially if I bring in a friend to help set the scene. Even if we don't go through with the surrogacy plan, I think it's something I'll be arranging for them soon. I know just the pair to call about setting it up too.

"I think we can work something out, pup. If we decide to go ahead with the surrogacy arrangement once you do your research about everything it will entail, do you want me to include you in the planning? Or shall I surprise you?"

"Surprise me, please?" They flash me their pleading eyes, a look that they've long since learned is impossible for me to resist. "If you don't mind handling the logistics?"

"I can do that. I'll coordinate with the doctors, Jared, and Logan for you, if that makes this easier. My pup loves surprises, don't you?" I croon as I gently pinch their cheeks, jiggling their face from side to side.

"Yep." Quent wriggles, like they're trying to wag a tail they aren't currently wearing. "Can we have playtime now, Mommy? I don't want to think about it anymore."

That's something I'll need to monitor; they need to grieve their loss and process everything surrogacy will require from them. But if it's easier to cope with everything in their pupspace for now, I am happy to facilitate that.

"Sure. That's enough serious talk for one day. Go down to the kennel so we can play. Have you eaten yet?"

"Nup." Quent shakes their head before dashing down the hallway to the door to our play area in the finished basement. They dance impatiently on all fours, pawing at the door when I take too long to gather up a box of their favorite cereal. They're already slipping into pup mode. It wouldn't surprise me if they struggle to stay in that headspace more than usual tonight, with everything we just discussed. Then again, Q can be alarmingly good at pushing down their emotions for someone who wears their heart on their sleeve. Especially in their pupspace.

"I'm coming, silly pup. Mommy needs to get your dinner."

Q barks playfully when I rattle the cereal that stands in for puppy kibble when we play. Sometimes I give them other treats, but this is an easy meal that helps them stay in their pupspace. So I've made peace with giving them a dinner that's mostly made of sugar occasionally.

I don't like them taking the stairs on all fours, so I prefer to wait to start our play when we're down there. Harry added carpeting and wider treads when we remodeled, but I still worry. Since Q is already in the zone, I give them the command to take the stairs on two legs. Q whines about it, but they comply, sitting and whining for a treat when they reach the bottom.

"Good, pup. Let's start by getting you into your gear." I gesture for them to heel and they trot obediently at my side over to our toy shelf, where I select a belted tail and a hood with fuzzy ears. We don't bother with stripping tonight. They press their face into the mask eagerly, licking at my hands and arms as I work the straps to fasten it into place. I know the foam snout will make it more difficult for the pup to eat, but that's part of the point. Q offers me each limb in turn so I can put on their paw mitts, boots, and knee pads. That just leaves the tail.

I run the belt around their hips, pausing to rub at their crotch until they whimper and moan for me. Q humps against my hand and spreads their legs to encourage me to touch them more. I consider getting them off to start our session, then think better of it. As long as their mind is on not being allowed to come, it won't be on the worries of their day. I move my hand, fastening the belt and arranging the fluffy gray tail to drape over their perky butt. It hangs between their legs. I grope the round curves of their ass, then step back to appraise my handiwork.

"There, that's my pretty pup." I nod in appreciation.

Q waggles their tail and turns to nuzzle their face against my crotch, snuffling loudly. I'm not in the mood to make this sexual tonight. Instead, I redirect the affection, pressing them close and rubbing them behind the ears before pointing to their basket of toys. "Go get your ball."

Q runs off to obey, nosing through the basket until they find their favorite soft blue ball. They bring it back and deposit the ball at my feet. I throw it, and they chase it across the softly padded floor. We play fetch until they're panting, sides heaving from running. They still drop the ball at my feet, looking at me expectantly. Their tummy rumbles.

"Dinner time. And I think you need to take a nice cool drink, hmm?"

Q barks an affirmative, then pants under the face mask. I scratch behind their ears and send them to put away their ball. While they're occupied, I get a bottle of water from the mini fridge we keep down here and retrieve their box of cereal. I get out their bowls, checking that both are clean from the last time we used them. Q saunters up to me on all fours and presses against the backs of my legs. I lean into their weight, eliciting a contented sigh from them. They nose at the bowls, so I back them up and make them sit.

"None of that. Manners, pup."

I give the command for them to wait while I fill both bowls. Q whines, but obeys. The hungry eyes they flash between me and their bowls are one of those looks that lets me know Q is still deep into a puppy headspace. They lick their chops, the tip of their tongue curling out from under their muzzle. Every muscle is tense as they await their release command. I set the bowls in a holder that puts it at a more ergonomic height for my human puppy before signaling that it's okay to eat.

Q falls on the food, pretty much exactly like a ravenous puppy as they gobble up their 'kibble' and lap their water. It will take them a while to get their fill with their mask impeding the process.

I go sit in my armchair and scroll on my phone, watching out of the corner of my eye while they eat. If I didn't know better, the sounds of Q snuffling in their bowl are pretty much exactly what it would sound like if they were a bio dog.

Eventually, Q pads over to me, rubbing their slobbery muzzle over my thighs and resting their chin in my lap. Their entire body waggles, making the limp tail flop behind them. They nose at my arm until I give them a thorough scratch. They shift their weight, like they want to jump up onto the chair with me. There isn't really room for that though. We can cuddle in bed later.

"Lay down." Q curls up at my feet with a satisfied sigh. I lean down to offer them their favorite chewie. It's a semi-hard silicone bone in blue, pink, and white. Q takes it and wedges one end between their front paws to gnaw on it. I tuck one foot under their belly and absently pet along the length of their back with the bare toes of the other. Meanwhile, I finish reading through my emails on my phone.

Q seems perfectly content at my feet. The rubbery squishes of the toy when they worry it in their mouth punctuate the silence.

I play a few rounds of solitaire to let them stay in their pupspace until they are ready to go upstairs. I've won four games when Q gets restless, shifting around and chewing more emphatically on the toy.

"Ready for bed?" I ask.

Q yips.

"Shall we take off the gear for bedtime or leave it on?"

Q whines when I reach for the straps, so I leave it for now and let them brave the stairs on all fours. Up presents less of a problem than down and the thick carpet on the treads makes the edges easier on my pup's knees, even when they aren't wearing their pads. They wait for me to open the door, then lead the way up a second flight of stairs to our bedroom. Q jumps into our bed and curls up on my pillow.

I laugh and shake my head as they watch me like they belong there. "You know that's not your spot, Q."

Q gives me a wide puppy grin and a tail wag. Their focus remains glued to me as I change into my pajamas. Their tongue lolls out under the muzzle and they look very pleased with themself. I don't make them move until I'm ready for bed, then I shove them onto their side of the mattress and get comfy under the covers. Q snuggles into my arms, licks across my mouth, and settles in next to me with a sigh.

It's not long before they bury their face in my neck and I feel the hot moisture of their tears. I expected this. For the emotions to hit them hard as they come back from their pup side. I hold them tight and murmur soothing words. "It's alright, I've got you. Let it all out, pup."

"He's gone." Quent gasps through big, body-wracking sobs. "Thomas is gone." The crying jag lasts a long time, Quent crying so hard they sometimes gasp for air alarmingly. They let me take off the face mask then, revealing a tear-streaked visage still twisted with sorrow and fear. I don't let go of them; their pain hurts my heart, and by the end we're both a blubbering mess. They cry themself into an exhausted sleep in my arms.

Once I'm sure they're out, I remove their knee pads and paw mitts, setting them aside on Quent's pillow. Quent dozes through the process and I take care not to disturb their peaceful slumber.

I hate that they had such a rough evening, but I love the way they can give themself to me like this. They came home tangled up in knots, worried about my reaction to their latest rash decisions, and not ready to face their grief. Yet they could give all of that to me, at least for the space of an evening.

They let themselves feel their fear and sorrow in the safety of my arms. It's always humbling to realize I've somehow won their complete trust. Quent knows I'll always take care of them and give them what they need.

Even during our stormiest patches, there's nothing in the world quite like getting to love on my pup. I thrive on being the one to keep them together when everything gets too overwhelming. I suspect that if we go through with their plans, I'm going to be holding on for dear life over the next several months.

CHAPTER 3

Quent

Mommy doesn't waste any time getting the ball rolling for me with the surrogacy thing. She gives me the weekend to think, and we read articles about it together. I don't bring it up with Jared next time we talk. Logan asks if I meant it, and I tell him I did and that Mommy will be in touch about the details. He agrees to handle their end of things with her.

Monday morning, when I haven't changed my mind, she calls to make an appointment with our doctor to ensure it's medically feasible for us as soon as possible. She doesn't express any more doubts about my decision. That isn't how things work for us. She trusts me to know myself as much as I trust her to take care of me. I am scared about this entire process though.

I'm never a fan of going to the actual doctor. Medical scenes at the club with Doc are way more fun. It's better now that we have a queer friendly primary care provider, but it's hard to shake off years of terrible experiences. When I was first trying to access transition related care, it was hard to find a competent provider. Let alone one who accepted me being nonbinary.

Not to mention the tribulations of getting a doctor to take me seriously to get my thyroid issues diagnosed. They all wanted to blame my hormone therapy or tie it into my being trans. I spent way too long dealing with constant fatigue and a slew of other unpleasant symptoms. The final straw that made me push for a diagnosis was the return of heavy, painful periods. That was despite my IUD and weekly testosterone shots rendering periods a thing of the past up to that point.

I had practically every doctor at my old clinic brush me off or suggest treating the separate symptoms before we switched providers and I got a thyroid test. And just like that, a simple daily pill fixed most of my issues. Sort of. It took time to figure out the right dose, but hormones are devious little fuckers. They can make you feel like a million bucks when they're right and dog shit when they're off. Lucky for me, my current doctor took the time to get the dosing right.

Doctor visits still make me anxious. Even when it's for something I want. Like when I got on testosterone. And when I went along with Mommy as her support person, so I'd know what sort of help she would need after her surgical procedures.

I guess that makes it sort of funny that I work in a medical profession as a pharmacy technician. But at least at the pharmacy, we actually take the time to listen to our patients when they come in with concerns. They come to the pharmacy with all kinds of questions you would think a doctor would answer. And yet, my bosses are the ones they trust to come to for advice. Guess I'm not the only one who's had unpleasant experiences.

Anyway, Mommy put her foot down and said that the first step to getting me knocked up is seeing our doctor. So that's what we're doing today, less than two weeks after I first made my offer to Jared. I am serious about surrogacy, so I guess Ky's right that we need to be sure of the potential risks and check out my general health first. I still don't like it, but I go along with the appointment. Mommy holds my hand while our doctor pokes and prods me and writes up a requisition for blood tests. She keeps holding my hand as we sit through a giant medical jargon laced info dump.

I tune out most of the details. I can ask Mommy or Fran from work for the big take home points, if I need a refresher. Most important is that I have to stop testosterone until after the birth. And when I get pregnant, I'll need to have my thyroid levels monitored and might need a higher dose of my meds. No big deal. Not compared to the benefit of getting to help Jared grow his family. Now that it's out there, I want to just hurry and get it over with.

The appointment is a big mental drain. We pick up a couple pints of ice cream on the way home from the lab where they draw my blood. Mommy indulges my sweet tooth most of the time, but I'd make myself sick to my stomach with sugary treats if left to my own devices. So one of our rules is that I need permission for treats. Plus, I prefer having to ask her. It makes me feel owned in the best way. Safe and cared for and treasured. And I'm all of those things with her. So the ice cream goes in the freezer when we get home from our appointments and shopping.

I try to behave myself while she works for a few hours. I had the day off from the pharmacy, but she still has clients to deal with and websites to design. Around suppertime, Jax comes over with his laptop and I order Thai delivery for dinner since I don't feel like cooking and Mommy is busy.

When Connor calls to complain about another in a long string of bad dates, I'm already considering which of the ice cream flavors to attack after I finish my noodles. I'm in a weird, restless mood. I invite him over as a distraction from thoughts of doing something naughty to get Mommy's attention.

It's not rational to want to lash out. I know she has to finish her projects, and she already spent most of the day doing things for and with me. But I'm frustrated. Mostly at the amount of waiting involved in my plans. I want to call Jared up and say I'll give him a baby and he can have it ASAP. But I can't just wave a magic wand and make my body cooperate with that vision of the future.

I have to wait for all my craptastic hormones to adjust to not getting my usual T injections. Then we hope my ovaries remember what they're supposed to do before we can even start trying. I hate, hate, hate waiting. And then there is waiting to ovulate, waiting to test, waiting for the baby to grow and be born. Wait, wait, wait. They've already waited for years. I don't want to make them wait more, but that's the only option.

So while I wait to start a ball rolling that is going to change everything, I wait for food delivery. And for Mommy to fix Jax's website, and for Connor to come over. Far too much waiting. It all makes me grumpy.

The food gets there a bit before Connor. He looks sad when he arrives, and his takeout burger looks even sadder. My noodles may or may not be kosher. Pretty sure they put shellfish in a lot of the sauces, or something. But I got the noodles with the vegetarian symbol by it on the menu, so that usually means it's okay to share with him. And the bean patty on his TV tray is sad, soggy and cold. I scoop a bunch of veggies and noodles out to feed to him and he accepts, taking the excuse of sharing to snuggle closer to me.

I enjoy having him here to take my mind off stuff, and he seems like he needs a distraction too. We watch a show about superheroes, both of us interjecting with backseat hero-ing of our own. When the noodles are gone, Mommy is still in her office with Jax.

I scowl at the closed office door and decide to earn myself a punishment. Ice cream time. Connor gives me a look that says he knows I'm not allowed treats without permission, but he isn't about to interfere if I want to get in trouble. Which I do. That's part of the fun with having rules. And blatantly breaking them like this will tell Mommy that I'm in a mood and I need her without my having to say anything outright. The talking can come after.

I huff out a sigh. I know I'm in a rough place when I'm already justifying my actions in my head. Ugh, I should have told Ky I wasn't okay after the appointment, but she needed to get work done and I didn't want to need the extra attention. My stomach shouldn't still be in knots hours after the appointment. I shouldn't feel ready to crawl out of my skin with nerves and the need to *do* something.

It was just a doctor's visit. She only removed my IUD and told me to stop taking my testosterone. And prescribed a prenatal vitamin. We didn't buy the bottle with a curvy lady on the label, but seeing it didn't help my mood at the store. No, the preview of all the misgendering to come made my stomach drop. At the same time, the fact I pushed past that moment, all those uncomfortable moments because I know this is something I have to do, only hardened my resolve. I can do this. One step at a time.

Connor snuggles closer to me when I sigh, his thigh against mine helps to still my nervous foot jiggling. He seems like he could use a sugary pick me up too. And I've been there. Before I met Mommy, I was certain I'd never meet anyone who gets me and my quirks the way she does. It's hard to date when you've got glaring differences to disclose. A treat will help us both bury our troubles in sweetness. So we share my mint chip ice cream until Mommy and Jax come out of the office.

Mommy takes one look at the two of us cozy on the couch in the den, and I know I'm in for it. I follow the script of a naughty pup caught breaking the rules, but on the inside I'm buzzing with anticipation and the conversation floats over me. Mommy makes sure our guests are okay with us disappearing for a bit, and then I'm ordered to our room. That's where the actual conversation will happen.

This was just me acknowledging that I broke the rules, but we won't dig into the meat of my problem in front of guests. Not even Connor, who I adore. What I need to say, and can't quite figure out how to put into words, is only for her ears. Something to be shared between the two of us in private.

I leave the ice cream with Connor. He still looks like he could use it. At least Jax is here to keep him company. The two of them might hit it off if they have a few minutes to interact outside of a scene. I hope so. We're going to be upstairs for a while. My emotions are like an angry ball of worms in the pit of my stomach.

Mommy follows me to our room. I drag my feet as we approach our door, dreading the look of disappointment that I'll get for not telling her what I need.

"If you wanted a spank, you could've just asked, Q." Mommy sounds exasperated.

"Oh, sure. Should I have barged into your office to ask for it in front of your client?" I snipe back. Inside, I cringe at taking that tone with her. It's not her fault I got all emotionally constipated after the appointment that she set up for me. I clench my fists so I won't shake. I'm a mess right now and we both know it.

Mommy rubs her temples, but keeps her composure, tone calm and collected. Everything I'm not as I shake with nerves in front of her. "I asked if you were alright after the appointment."

"And I was." I take a deep breath and try to match her calm. "Or I thought I could handle it. But then I had all afternoon to think and I just want to do it already."

"Do it, huh?" She arches a brow at me, not rising to my bait. She gives me space to just spew out my emotions to her. And her patience is the key that unlocks the floodgates. All my fear and impatience tumbles out of me as I find the words to explain what has me so on edge tonight.

"Yeah. I want it, but I also want it to be over. All the unknowns and the entire process terrifies me. The waiting, and wondering if it's physically possible makes me anxious. I'm worried about whether I'll have stretch marks or if my chest will puff up like a water balloon and if it will ever go back to how it was. What if something goes terribly wrong with me or the baby? I want to fast-forward past all that. Like in those alien movies where they wake up and discover 'surprise! There is a weird life-form already fully gestated and ready to burst forth from your body.' And then they have the baby parasite pretty much the same day they find out it's in there. Poof. Done." I gesture wildly.

Mommy snorts. "That isn't how human biology works."

"I know. Dogs only gestate for two months," I grumble, sounding like nothing so much as a sullen child.

"You aren't a bio canine, Quent. You know you don't have to do this." She softens as she steps closer to me.

I let her cup my cheek in her palm, nuzzling into her touch. "Ugh. I know. But I want to. I just want it to be something I can do, get done, and put behind me. Why can't reality skip to the part where Jared and Logan are calling for us to babysit because they're exhausted from being up all night with the kid? I'm terrible at waiting."

I step away and pace at the foot of our bed as I rant out my frustrations. Pacing helps, lets me channel all the frenetic energy that's been roiling inside me since we got home. This is good. Talking it out with her is what I should have done instead of sneaking treats. I needed to talk to her about this.

"I hadn't noticed," Mommy says, dry as dust. She doesn't say more, letting the silence draw out anything else I'm hiding.

I fidget, toying with my collar before opting to change the subject. "What's my punishment for sneaking treats?"

"You aren't getting one." Mommy crosses her arms over her chest. She's extra hot when she's firm with me like this.

"But I broke the rules." I whine. "Downstairs you said I'd get one."

Mommy nods. "You broke the rules to get a punishment. So your punishment is not getting what you want."

I pout. Mommy reaches for me. She hooks a finger through my collar and pulls me close for a kiss, just a peck on the lips before she rests her forehead against mine. "If we're doing this, I need you to talk to me, pup."

I sigh. "I'll try to do better. It's been a weird day."

"I understand that. Is it just about the waiting?" She cuts to the heart of my anxiety.

"Yeah. I think so? I don't know. The whole, waiting for my body to go back to how it was before hormones is kind of blah? Like, it has a bit of that creeping dread vibe? But also, most of the changes that matter the most to me aren't just going to reverse overnight or probably at all. I'll still be me. Just with functioning ovaries. I hope."

"You'll still be you no matter what, Quentin." She rubs my arms reassuringly.

I nod. "I'll still be me with a big fat belly full of baby too. And if my chest, uh, develops."

"You will." She licks her lips and glances down at my body.

"And you'll like me with big tits, won't you?" I tease, because I know she will. Not that she isn't into my boyishly flat chest as things stand, just that I've also seen her porn preferences.

"I love you, no matter how you look, Q."

"Sure, but like, will you be disappointed if I decide to have them reduced after? Even just a tiny bit?" I hold up my fingers pinched together in emphasis. The teasing is a thin veneer over my fears.

Ky tugs on my collar again, a reminder that I'm hers. She waits until our eyes lock to say, "I will never be upset about you doing what's best for you. It's your body to make those choices about." It sounds so mushy. But it's exactly what I need to hear. That she loves me unconditionally, and she respects that this is something I have to do.

"And my choice is usually to let you do whatever you want with it." I press up against her, unspeakably relieved to have this all out in the open. I might not be getting the punishment I thought I wanted, but this is better. A confirmation that Mommy knows me and will always give me what I need, even when I can't quite articulate it.

"Mhm." She slips a hand under my shirt to tweak one of my nipples. "I think we make excellent choices about this body together. What do you think?"

"Yeah." I agree, arching into her touch. "We do."

"Tonight, you're going to wear your chastity. So you can remember who you belong to and who you come to with a problem instead of acting out to get my attention."

"Yes, Mommy."

"Are you staying in the guest room with Connor or joining me in our bed?"

I hesitate. I want to sleep in Mommy's arms, but Connor could probably use a good cuddle as much as me tonight. "Um, I might cuddle with Connor until he falls asleep."

"Yeah?"

"Yeah. Because he's my friend and he needs me, but I want to sleep with you after."

"That's my good pup. Let's get you locked up so we don't leave Con waiting alone for too long."

I consider who we left my best friend downstairs with. Something tells me they might benefit from a chance to get better acquainted. I dawdle about retrieving the chastity belt. It's something we got modified to cup my junk comfortably while still keeping it off limits. It's perhaps not shocking that most of the typical chastity gear doesn't quite work for me. Designs for outies rely on having balls to lock around and designs for innies chafe on my bottom growth. So, we went custom for the device stashed at the back of my upstairs toy drawer.

Chastity is not my favorite punishment. Mommy laughs whenever I remind her of that fact. Apparently, I'm not meant to enjoy it. But I like how the belt is a constant reminder that I belong to Mommy when she makes me wear it. All of me, even the parts she doesn't mind me sharing with people outside our relationship.

Sometimes, I like when she exerts her control like this. Reminds me that our arrangement exists because it makes us both happy and not because she isn't interested in owning me in a sexual way. She's still the one I want to belong to, no matter who I'm fucking. Or being fucked by. And presenting myself to her to buckle the belt into place is a nice tangible reminder of her claim on me.

Mommy follows my lead in going slow with the straps. She cinches the belt tight, pressing a kiss to my bare skin above the waistband. "You're taking this calmly."

I reach reflexively for my collar. "I love knowing I'm yours."

"You're always mine." She gives the heart-shaped ring in the front a gentle tug.

"Yeah." I agree, swallowing hard against the soft pressure on my throat.

"Don't you want to get back to our guests?" Mommy prompts as she fastens the belt's little lock in place. She tucks the key into her pocket of her skirt, ensuring I won't be getting free until she is ready to release me. I know where the spare is, so if I had an emergency where I needed it off, I could do it, but that's hardly the point.

"Or...we could let Jax and Connor talk while we make out for a bit," I suggest hopefully.

"Are you trying to play matchmaker?" Mommy arches a finely sculpted brow at me.

"Maybe? Jax is good with littles. And I bet Con would have better dating luck with someone who gets what it's like to be trans. Also, I want him to find someone here so that he won't move back to the boonies and stop being my friend." I pout, because I've seen how much Connor misses his family and I don't want to lose my best friend. So if that means shameless matchmaking to keep him close, well, I can't be held responsible for at least trying. Besides, Jax is someone who I think would make Connor laugh.

"How very devious of you to invite them both over tonight, puppy." Mommy chuckles, shaking her head at my none too subtle scheming. She presses the heel of her hand against the front of my belt. Her touch applies pressure all around the area where I want it without giving me any of the friction I crave.

"Please?" I hump fruitlessly against her hand.

"It's almost like you want me to torture you, pup." Mommy kisses my throat, the sort of sucking kiss that goes right to my groin.

I groan and tip my face up for her to kiss me properly. "Yes. I love when you torment me, Mommy."

Mommy kisses my lips, pressing harder on my belt, until it

digs in just this side of the bad kind of pain. "Be careful what you wish for, Quentin." The heat in her gaze has lust pooling in my belly. I whine hungrily for more. "You want to show Mommy what a devoted pup you are, Q? Keep me busy, so your scheming has time to work?"

"Yes, please," I agree.

"Down." Mommy accompanies the command with a gesture. Her tone brooks no argument. I drop to my belly, letting myself fall into my pupspace as I wriggle closer to her. I crawl forward like a bio dog eager to greet my beloved human. Mommy lets me approach, but doesn't otherwise acknowledge me at her feet. I whine, hoping for pets and lick my chops submissively.

She nudges the toe of her boot against my chin. I glance up at her and whine my request, I'd wag my tail, if I had one attached. The sort of hopeful wag that's just asking for her approval.

"Lick." She presses more firmly, and I don't have to be asked twice. I lap at the toe of her boot, the rich taste of leather pleasant on my tongue. Mommy doesn't move and I lavish attention on the toe of the boot, licking methodically over every inch. Showing her I'm hers to command, no matter how degrading it might seem. I mouth at the toe and she tuts her disapproval, the loud click of her tongue startling me into stopping. "Did I say suck?"

I whine and go back to licking, letting myself get lost in the smoothness of the supple leather under my tongue. This is pure obeisance to my Mommy, the joyful acknowledgement of her utter and complete ownership of me, and I love it.

I whine low, plaintive sounds, seeking reassurances.

Mommy murmurs back with occasional praise. "Just like that." When I lathe hard at a scuffed patch near her ankle. "Don't miss a single spot, pup." When I miss the bit at the heel and have to bow low and press my face against the carpet to get the heels.

"Keep going. Show me who owns you." When I tire, slowing my efforts.

Mommy lets me slobber all over her foot. She swivels her ankle to give me access to the arch of her instep, the top of the boot, the heel, and up the rise of the ankle. I lick until my mouth aches, and then I keep going, glancing up for her continuing approval.

Mommy eventually withdraws her foot and presses the other against my lips. We repeat the entire process until I've got both boots shiny with spit. When she's satisfied with my treatment of the tops of her shoes, she lifts her first boot and presses the sole against my cheek.

"You're going to clean the entire thing, aren't you, puppy?"

I whine and wriggle agreeably. She applies enough pressure to squish my cheek against the ground.

"You worship the ground Mommy walks on, don't you, pup?"

I whine my agreement again.

"Prove it." She steps back, sitting on the edge of our bed. I belly crawl after her and wait for her to offer me her boots again. This time she presses the sole of her boot against my face and I lick that just as dutifully as I did the tops.

The rubber doesn't taste nearly as good as the leather bits. It's rough against my tongue, the treads scraping my already abused mouth. And even though these boots aren't a pair that she wears outside our house, the idea of licking the ground she's walked on is debasing in a wonderfully arousing way.

I grind my locked up bits against my own ankle ineffectually as Mommy encourages me to work my tongue over the soles of her boots. It makes me want to whine, growl, or beg for release, but this isn't about me, so I grind harder to ride out the frustration and keep licking. This part always makes me feel so small and owned and perfectly hers.

It's trust, and ceding all control. Obedience and adoration. Humiliation and pride in her ownership. Debasement and utter complete love. It's worshiping my Mommy with my mouth and knowing that she loves me enough to give me this degradation that I need. It's taking everything from me, down to my dignity, each of us wanting and needing the same thing in photo-negative. She gives me all of her as much as I've given myself to her.

Mommy leans forward to rest her hand on the top of my head. Her touch grounds me as she presses my mouth against the bottom of her boot and it makes me feel treasured as much as I'm owned. I whimper as I lap at the rubber treads, desperate to show her I'm all hers, no matter how tired my mouth is.

I adore her, right down to the soles of her boots. The cute custom-sized boots that cover a part of her that causes her dysphoria even post-transition. She told me once that having me lick her boots is a way of saying fuck you to the idea her feet make her less femme. A reminder to herself that every part of her is lovable, and I'm showing my whole-hearted agreement to her with every swipe of my tongue. I love every bit of her.

"Good pup. That's enough. Up on the bed."

I blink at her in a daze when she pulls her foot away. I'm not sure when she rucked up her skirt and pushed her panties down enough to finger herself, but she did. My brain is still stuck on licking, so I curl my tongue over my lips a few times before I marshall the will to stop on command. I want to be licking her bare flesh.

Mommy stands and gazes down at me, affection in her eyes, but she already gave me her next command and when I don't obey, she nudges me with her toe. "Come get your belly rubs, pup. You've earned a reward. You wouldn't want to spoil it now with disobedience, would you?"

Right. On the bed. I hop up and flop down on my back, legs drawn up to give her access, even though she's already locked my sensitive bits away. "Tip your head back, off the edge of the mattress. Mouth open, tongue out."

I wriggle into position and Mommy steps up to press her clit against my tongue. Her silky panties must have slipped down her legs when she stood, since they aren't in my way. It takes every ounce of my self-control not to start licking again. I stay where I am while she rubs against me. The hem of her skirt tickles my cheeks when she lets it drape over my face. The heady taste of her makes me ache for more than I'm going to be getting.

"Give Mommy kisses, Q." Mommy croons the command I'm waiting for. I go to town on her clit, suckling on the sensitive little nub until she takes back control. Mommy presses my face into her folds so I can really eat her out. Much as my friends like to joke about my love of bones, I enjoy eating pussy equally as much.

Basically, putting my lover in my mouth always makes me feel good. There isn't much better than using my mouth to bring a lover to the brink. And that goes double with Mommy. I love the high-pitched, almost involuntary sounds she makes when I pleasure her. The way her breath hitches when I lap at her folds and find the perfect spot to drive her wild. I love the taste of her, the rich feminine musk that coats my tongue.

I love her, and I make love to her until my jaw aches and my little cock is pulsing with need in its cage. Even with no friction, I could probably get off from having Mommy in my mouth like that. She's using me, forcing my mouth against her and taking all control while giving me my favorite sex act, and it's glorious. I only need a little more to push me past the brink, a little more of her control. If she gives me any stimulation, I'll come despite the bondage on my T-dick. Oh, please, just a little more.

I moan around her clit and that's enough to tip Mommy over

the edge; she rides out the orgasm for what feels like an eternity, rocking against my face, hips moving in a sinuous dance, abs tight as the pleasure overtakes her entire body.

Please. I don't beg or change what I'm doing; I don't want to disrupt her enjoyment. But I need her so desperately. Need so much for her to touch me and take me over the edge with her. And then she does. Tweaking my nipples hard as she grinds her clit into my tongue.

I arch and come too. My orgasm is almost painful with nothing touching my T-dick. The need to bury myself in something is a powerful ache that unfurls through my groin. It has me bucking my hips up off the bed until Mommy grips them and pins them down. Oh, fuck, that bit of restraint, knowing I don't have control, sends me to some transcendent place. Where everything seems to center on that single point of pleasure crashing down around me and exploding outward.

The orgasm subsumes everything until I'm a panting, trembling puddle in my Mommy's arms. I'm not entirely sure how I went from hanging my head off the edge of the mattress to cradled against her chest in a pillow nest. Regardless of the how, I'm boneless and content to rest there in the afterglow for a while. We eventually have to go back downstairs to check on our guests.

When we return to the den, Connor looks sheepish about finishing my ice cream. Or maybe it's the wet patches on his pants and shirt and the sudden disentangling of their limbs he and Jax did when we walked in on them.

Jax looks like the cat who caught the canary, so I'm pretty sure re-introducing them was as good an idea as I thought it would be. I pretend not to notice the dampness on Connor's clothing. Or the kiss-swollen look to Jax's lips. Connor offers me the same consideration, not commenting on my freshly fucked appearance.

Jax makes his excuses and leaves, but I catch the longing glance he throws back over his shoulder at Connor. Too bad Con is totally oblivious to the want in Jax's eyes. Connor looks all morose, staring at the blank TV screen, so I plop down practically in his lap and draw him in for some snuggles. "Hold me." I demand imperiously. That makes him smile, even if it doesn't quite reach his eyes.

Mommy makes us popcorn and joins us, making it pretty much the perfect evening.

I know Mommy would rather watch one of her heartfelt indie films that put me to sleep. That makes it mean even more to me when she valiantly sits through Connor and my choice without a word of complaint. Mommy lets us enjoy our over the top superhero antics in peace. I make a mental note to return the favor with a movie night to watch her latest favorites.

Mommy and Connor both pet me absently as we watch TV. I soak up all the touches. This totally makes up for having to see the doctor earlier. I got to worship Mommy and now I get to cuddle with two of my favorite people while we watch a few more episodes of our show before bed. Epic win.

CHAPTER 4

Quent

The chemical aftertaste of a condom lingers on my tongue as I follow obediently along at Mommy's heels. We're at Adventures to play and I welcome the chance to lose myself in some scenes. I've been antsy to get the surrogacy show on the road ever since my period returned last week.

That should mean we can start trying to knock me up, but Mommy hasn't mentioned any solid plans for that yet. It has me on edge, wondering if we're still on to do it. I'm too conscious that the subject is a raw wound for my brother for me to bring it up with him when we talk.

Our play tonight is a welcome distraction from everything in my life I can't control. It's technically Littles Night, but pet players and our handlers are welcome too, since most of the club's littles love to play with pets.

The public play area is an open expanse broken up by an eclectic mix of furniture. Couches for aftercare snuggles, spanking benches for play, that sort of thing. There's also a makeshift stage for demos, or folks who want more of an audience. It's all a touch shabby and dated, but it's a second home to us regulars and I'm comfortable being myself here.

Martin, the club owner, keeps the more specialized furniture and toys in the themed private rooms that line the outer walls of the area. Tonight, a cleared space in the middle of the room holds some low tables where several of the club's littles are coloring. Martin also brought out some bins of toys and a couple of area rugs with car tracks on them. Like what you might find in a nursery rolled out for the specialty night.

Mommy is leading me toward one of the private rooms. Since we arrived early, she let me have a treat. The best kind of treat, sucking off one of my friends. Monty's moans of pleasure are still ringing in my ears and the delicious stretch of his hard dick filling my mouth is still satisfying. That perfect fullness, the thrill of being responsible for another person's pleasure, has me aroused as all hell and floating somewhere that isn't quite pupspace.

I want to paw at myself, but Mommy told me she has plans for tonight. Big plans and something exciting to tell me. I want my surprise. So I refrain from breaking the rules about touching myself without her permission when we're playing.

Most of the time, she doesn't mind if I take care of myself when I get horny. The 'horny pup who humps everything' act that I sometimes indulge in even gets a chuckle out of her when we're at home in our playroom. But when she lets me play with other people, my pleasure belongs one hundred percent to her. I belong to her and that's one small way I can show it.

Mommy leads me to the private room with the medical equipment. Her hand brushes my nape because I'm pressed so close to her side as we walk. I want to feel owned tonight. She pauses before opening the door and I crowd close to her side, all but sitting on her feet when she gives me a sit cue. I nuzzle into her hand and whine at the delay.

"You nervous about seeing the vet, pup?" Mommy ruffles my hair. Her fingers muss my floppy puppy ears on the headband I'm wearing tonight before she clips my lead to the heart-shaped ring on my collar. And just like that, yeah, I am a little nervous about what she has in store for me.

I yip an affirmative and tug against her hold on my lead. Doc opens the door to the private room and greets Mommy with a smile before I can get too riled. I dart behind Mommy and press myself against her calves, like that might hide me from the man with the needles and the sharp medical scent in the room.

Doc, who has played the role of vet with us in the past, chuckles. "I see Q remembers me from our last appointment."

"That they do." Mummy tugs me out from behind her and I whine at being forced toward the door. My paws slip across the smooth flooring, unable to get any purchase as Mommy scoots me into the room with her hands on my flanks. She shuts the door on my half-formed escape plans and crouches down to eye level. I want to growl in frustration, but that might get me reprimanded. I don't want to be a naughty pup tonight, so I give her my best pleading eyes and whine pitifully.

Mommy takes my face in her hands and gives me kisses. She calls me her good brave pup until I can all but forget whatever nefarious plot she has cooked up with Doc. I wriggle my ass to make my tail wag as I lick her face back. She laughs when my tongue finds her mouth. Mommy holds me still to give me one last kiss before she gives the hand signals for me to sit and stay. I take up the requested position and watch as she talks to Doc.

"Let's get your pup up on the table and we can begin with a physical." He pats the crinkly paper on the exam table. I cringe at the unexpected noise.

I don't want to get up on the table. The sharp tang of antiseptic reminds me of the last time I was here. Needles. Doc likes needle play and Mommy likes to watch and fuss over me after, but it's not my favorite type of scene. Not a hard limit, but a soft one and part of what makes it bearable for me is being coddled and coaxed into going along with it. I hope it isn't needles today. That's been the best part of going off my testosterone prescription for the past three months. Maybe the only good part. I could get used to the lack of needles in my life.

"Come here, pup." Mommy snaps her fingers for me to follow her. I dig in my heels and she drags me toward the table with her hands under my armpits. I break free before she can lift me onto the exam table.

She grabs for me, but I whine and dodge. Her lunge to recapture me lets me pull the leash free. Doc and Mommy both chase me around the room, which is fun until Mommy wraps me in a bear hug and lifts me up onto the crinkly paper covering the padded bench. I squirm in her grasp, but not enough to risk making her drop me. I enjoy being forced like this. When Mommy picks me up like I really am her feisty terrier puppy, it makes me glad that I'm small enough for her to overpower physically sometimes.

Mommy deposits me on the table on all fours and gives my nose a firm bop. "No more of that or you'll be in trouble later, Q. Mommy doesn't want you to fall off the table and hurt yourself."

That's fair. I don't struggle, and I give my tail a single wag to let her know I'm done fighting. Mommy doesn't take her restraining hands off me, though, too wise to my tricks to be lulled into complacence. She rubs my ears.

"You good, pup?" That's a cue to let her know if I'm still okay with this. A check in. It pulls me away from just being a pup, but it's reassuring to know I have an out. I lick her hand, letting her know I still want to play without having to shift mental gears. She slips her fingers under my collar to rub at my neck, reminding me I'm hers and she's here if I need her. I relax at that touch. Mommy has me and nothing too bad will happen to me while she's here.

The paper crinkles when I shift my weight, but I don't react to it, watching Mommy for any new cues. Doc waits until I've calmed to approach.

"Shall we discuss what brings you in today?" Doc pulls on a pair of latex gloves. He stands on the other side of the table from Mommy so she can hold me while he takes my face between his hands and starts feeling me all over. Pressing into my neck like he's feeling my lymph nodes or something. "I believe they're due for a shot."

That makes me tense. I prefer to do my shots at home. It's usually something Mommy does for me when I'm not in my pupspace, but sometimes it's part of our scenes with Doc. I whimper and shuffle my paws on the crinkly paper. He's going to give it to me in the butt and I'll be sore for a while after. I know he's actually trained to do injections for his job. Usually, if he gives me a shot, the meds are my weekly testosterone prescription. I trust him and my Mommy. But I don't like the idea of having to get a shot that I don't need. Even if it is harmless saline.

Mommy ruffles my hair. "What's the matter? You don't want your shots, pup?"

I whine again, nosing at Mommy's fingers plaintively.

"You're in luck, Q, no shots today." That pulls me up short and I freeze as she continues to caress me, fingers working behind my ears and along my nape. I'm curious where she and Doc are going with this setup to the scene.

"That's right. You mentioned you're thinking about breeding them." Doc rests a hand on my head.

Oh. Oh! I let out an excited yip and can't help wagging my tail at that. I hope that means what I think it means. Mommy promised me a big surprise tonight. Is this it? I struggle against Doc's grip on me to crane around and look at Mommy. I need to see her expression to judge if she really means it or if this is just a medical scene. So much for forgetting my worries, but I want it to mean we're moving ahead to the next step.

"That's right. You can't take your meds while you're growing a puppy for me, can you, Q? Might hurt the pup." She ruffles my hair. "I wanted to make sure my sweet little bitch is nice and healthy and up to date on their vaccinations first though." Mommy strokes a proprietary hand along my entire back and when I catch her eye, she gives me a quick nod. I try to lick her hand and she laughs as she pets my hair again. "You like that idea, huh, Q? You want Mommy to find a stud to breed you full of pups? Want to carry a litter for me?"

I whine and wriggle hard enough that my tail flops against my thighs as I move. Of course I like it. She's offering me my fondest desire. This one kink that is my go-to personal fantasy. The one I'd all but given up on ever trying for real because it's a limit for her. And now she's saying I can have it?

No, more than that, she's actively participating in the build-up. Along with excitement thrumming through my nerves and lust heating my blood at the images her dirty talk paints, I can't help all the questions bubbling up inside me. I need words for a minute. Details.

This is something she knows I've wanted for a while now. I can't play along if this is just an elaborate game. Or if she has any reservations about her part in the roleplay. Mommy wouldn't be cruel enough to tease me with this if it wasn't real. She wouldn't offer it if it would hurt her. I just need to hear her confirm all of that.

"Yellow."

Doc steps back from the table, deferring to Mommy. "Do you two need a minute to talk?"

"No. Just. For real? This isn't just a scene?" I sit up and look at Mommy eye-to-eye. Hope bubbles through me. I get to try a breeding scene and Mommy is so hot when she talks about it. I can't wait to hear her saying those filthy things to me while she's actually having me bred. Heat coils low in my belly at the thought of it. "You talked to Jar and Logan?"

"Yeah, baby, for real. They're ready to try, if you still want to be their surrogate?" She searches my face for signs of doubt. I'm sure though.

We've talked about what it will be like and I'm ready. Telling me she's ready to arrange things in a scene is perfect for us. In hindsight, she dropped some hints that she had news that I'd appreciate leading up to tonight's scene. She said I'd be getting a surprise and asked if I wanted hints about it, but I trust her not to spring anything I'll hate on me.

Even if it is the sort of news that we need to discuss further, and telling me something so monumental in a scene like this could backfire terribly. Mommy knows I'll safeword if I need to. She trusts me as much as I trust her. And I know we'll still discuss everything more after the scene ends.

But for now, I like the idea of Doc giving me a thorough exam as part of the process. As if this scene is a lead up to that one. It might be a good way to get around some of my nerves about the actual mechanics of the entire thing.

Being Mommy's good pup will make it easier to face the scary parts of this. She came with me to the appointment where my actual doctor cleared me to go off hormones and try to get pregnant. Mommy was the one who took notes and asked questions and made sure we had all the information we needed to decide how to do this.

Mommy always makes the scary things bearable for me. But then we did the preliminary steps and Jar and Logan didn't bring it up again and neither did Mommy. Now it's been months since I went off my meds. And a week since I got a period. We cracked jokes about our hormone cycles syncing up since we were both dealing with period bloat and a need for chocolate at the same time.

Mommy said she'd arrange the details with Logan and Jared for me, but she hasn't brought up the baby thing again until tonight. I sort of figured they might've changed their minds about wanting to go through with it. Or that they might not be ready to try again, yet. Part of me hoped they would call this off and let me off the hook. A small, scared part of me I'm not proud of. Hearing that they still want it fills me with equal parts dread over a potential pregnancy and excitement about finally taking action.

I've mostly been ignoring my doubts lately. Now they're roaring to life, at war with the giddy joy at Mommy agreeing to a breeding scene and everything this will mean for my brother. As much as it will mean to Jared and Logan, this will have consequences for Mommy and me too. Mommy says it's my choice, but I wasn't sure if she was really okay with this until now.

My eyes prickle with moisture. I'm not sure if the tears are happy, sad, or just plain overwhelmed, but I fling myself into her arms. She holds me and murmurs into my hair, petting me until I gather myself enough to get back into the scene. I can figure out exactly how I feel about this later. It's too much to sort out right now, and I crave the escape of cramming it all to the side as I return to my pupspace. When I'm ready, I pull free of her hold, shake myself, and turn back toward Doc.

"You good to go, Q?" Mommy checks.

I give her an affirmative yip. This role is a familiar retreat when life is too much to handle and I can slip into it with ease most of the time. Mommy doesn't take her comforting hand off my shoulder, but Doc steps back up to the table. He smiles. "There, ready for me to examine you, Q?"

I bark my agreement and he goes back to running his hands over my body as I let myself sink further into my pupspace. The scene helps. Doc keeps touching me in the detached, brusque way that makes this feel like a real vet check as he and Mommy discuss me over my head. What do I eat? How often do I potty? When was my last estrus?

It's all toe-curlingly intimate. I feel utterly degraded to have them talking about me and my body as if I'm not even there, or incapable of understanding. It's different from when I feel like I have to check my humanity at a human doctor's door. This is empowering because it's my choice to give up control. My choice to be Mommy's pup and trust in her judgment.

Doc's hands roam freely over my body as the two of them talk, pressing and prodding. It adds to the sense of being owned by my Mommy. Every part of me is hers to control. Hers is the only permission he needs to do whatever he wants to me. The humiliation and stimulation from being touched all over makes me hornier than I was when she shared me with Monty out in the public play area.

I try to hold still and be a good pup while Doc checks out my eyes, ears, and mouth. His blunt fingers probe along my gums, forcing my mouth open as he continues to talk to Mommy. He asks me to sit, then stand, and listens to my chest with his cold stethoscope. Doc lifts each of my legs to assess my range of motion. He probes my ass with his fingers. All of it is clinical and detached. Through it all, Mommy stands next to the exam table, watching impassively as she answers his questions.

"Now for the internal exam. We've got to make sure you've got room in there for puppies, right?" Doc positions me on the table with my ass up and my chest down. Mommy presses my face into the crinkly paper while Doc drizzles cold lube over my nether regions. Then he pushes his gloved fingers inside of me, probing around until he finds a spot that makes me buck and writhe into the touch. "Hm, well, your pup seems receptive. I need them to stop moving while I conduct the internal exam."

"Settle, pup, you heard the doctor." Mommy tugs on my collar.

I whine and he rubs me more firmly, pumping his fingers inside me and crooking them to stimulate me more. I try to stay still, but when he brushes his thumb over my external bits, I can't help bucking into his hand. It's just so good, the need to hump into the friction is overwhelming.

"I said settle. The vet needs to make sure you're healthy enough to breed." Mommy swats my ass gently. I try to obey while Doc fucks his fingers into me until I'm dripping and desperate to move and get more friction. My breath comes in hard pants with the effort of holding back. Mommy has a firm grip on my collar now, reminding me I'm hers to share like this. It's a wonderful torture, trying to not to move, every muscle tensing with the effort as pleasure sings along my nerves.

Mommy grips my collar tighter to pin me in place and I whine with need, begging her to let me have my release. Doc doesn't stop fingering me until I'm trembling with the effort not to come. I whimper and edge my face toward Mommy's chest.

"Does my pup need to come?" Mommy croons over the slick sounds of Doc's fingers pumping into me. I can only whine more and try to lick her face. She strokes my cheek. "Doc, what do you think? Has my pup earned a reward?"

"I think so. Q's a very responsive puppy." He presses harder with the finger circling my T-dick and pushes in deep, stretching me open. I whimper at how good it feels, hanging on by a thread while I wait for Mommy's command.

"Come, pup."

My entire body shudders with the force of my release. I ride Doc's fingers through the high and Mommy presses a kiss to my lips, swallowing the sounds of pleasure I make as I unravel.

Doc's presence fades to background noise when my Mommy tips my face up and demands that I open for her. She takes possession of me, kissing me like I belong to her and I'm hers to command. And I am. I'm hers completely and irrevocably. Mommy tugs on the collar that symbolizes her ownership of me again, and I shudder with another wave of pleasure at that reminder as Doc continues to stimulate me.

Mommy eventually ends the kiss, leaving me dazed and sprawled on the exam table. Doc pulls his gloved fingers out of me and presses them to my lips. I lick obediently, tasting myself and the nitrile gloves.

"I don't see any reason you can't get a litter or two out of them." He rubs affectionately behind my ears with his other hand as he talks to Mommy about getting me knocked up. I let the words roll over me like warm static. Nothing I need to worry about because Mommy is going to handle the details. The only thing I need to concern myself with is being her good pup.

Everything will be perfect and I can finally give something back to Jared for all the years he took care of me. For how he helped me to figure out who I am. I squash down the lingering doubts and fears, clinging instead to the post-orgasmic glow and the heady anticipation of the epic breeding scene Mommy agreed to give me. I am doing this and it's all going to be fine. Better than fine. It will all be perfect.

CHAPTER 5

Kylee

Q is flying high by the end of our session with Doc. We give Q a moment after they come. Not just because they need that time to settle, but because I enjoy loving on my pup. While they relax on the cushioned table, I savor the moment with them. I run my hands over their pliant body, taking the time to memorize them like this.

Q wants to do the surrogacy thing, but I know the coming changes are going to be hard for us both to handle. I want this memory of their total trust in me to help get us through the rough days ahead. They mean the world to me.

Doc spends a few minutes doting attention on my pup with me, and we debrief about the scene. I check in that he doesn't need us to stick around, but the scene wasn't particularly involved compared to what we usually do with him. It was mostly intense for Q because I dropped the news we're going to do the breeding scene they've wanted for a long time. Plus, letting them know I've made the arrangements for their surrogacy agreement with Logan and Jared must be emotional. It is for me too.

I debated how to bring it up, waffling over whether to discuss it prior to the scene first. In the end, I saved it for tonight because Q wanted to be surprised when I offered to tell them what I had planned for our evening. Even after I hinted that it was big news they might want to mentally prepare for. I'm glad they paused the scene to discuss it though. Even with as well as I know them, I can still miscalculate how much a scene will affect them.

When Q shivers on the table, Doc brings over a blanket to tuck around them and a bottle of water. My pup crowds closer to me and that's my cue to take them somewhere quiet for snuggles. I have to help them down off the exam table. They lean on me when they stand, the blanket still clutched around their shoulders.

"Thank the Doc, Quentin," I remind them, using a longer version of their full name to continue easing them out of the scene.

"Thanks, Doc," Quent parrots obediently.

"Anytime, Quent. And good luck with the surrogacy plans." Doc smiles at them.

"Thanks, Doc." Quent beams at the reminder that we're really doing it. They walk back out to the common area on shaky legs. I stay glued to their side until I have them settled on an out of the way couch at the edge of the room. We cuddle together there, with a view of others playing while they come down from the scene.

Quent crawls into my lap, straddling me and nuzzling into my chest. I tuck the blanket around their shoulders to keep them warm. This is the sweetness I love about aftercare. My cuddle-bug pressed close to my heart. Quent lets me embrace the role of maternal nurturer. Our dynamic is everything the little girl I used to be wanted in life, and grew up doubting I'd ever have.

"Thank you, Mommy. I needed that," Quent murmurs into my neck.

"You're very welcome, my sweet pup." I smooth my fingers through their hair and along their back to rest on their hips. They love to be touched as much as I love to touch them. Quent wriggles on top of me. In truth, I needed tonight too. I needed their surrender to my control of every part of them. An affirmation that they still trust me to guide and care for them, even when they are taking our life in a scary new direction.

I know they don't always love the vet play scenes we do. That's part of the appeal, knowing the Quent will accept my dominance even when it doesn't suit their wishes. I cherish their obedience even more when they are acting against their own preferences, when they let me push them right up to their limits.

Tonight didn't come close to their boundaries, but I suspect they are making a choice that will shove them far past their limits out of love for their brother. I'm afraid of what that will mean for us. More than anything, I'm not sure I'm strong enough to hold us together if they shut down and bury their fears and doubts as they are wont to do. Not when I suspect the pregnancy will be hard for me to watch.

It's inevitable that this will put a strain on our relationship. Will they want me to stop touching them as their body changes? Have they even considered how much we both need this physical intimacy? I press them closer to my chest, memorizing the warm weight of my love in my arms. Quent makes a sleepy sound of approval, nuzzling my neck.

I'm afraid they'll have a hard time telling me about their dysphoria, knowing that the source of it is something I'll never get to experience. Not that I particularly want children, but it's something I never had a choice about. If this works, in a matter of months, their body will undergo changes I'd celebrate, and it will make them miserable.

I wish I could be the one to do this for the people we love. Instead, Quent is giving up a piece of themself, and I don't know how I'm going to let go of that piece of them. We're going to be involved in our nibling's life. We already have regular get-togethers with Jared and Logan; the baby won't change that.

Jared and Logan promised us plenty of access to our future

nibling. It's part of the agreement we drew up. But that doesn't change the fact the baby the love of my life wants to carry—the one I'd never have asked them to have for us—is going to call me Aunty instead of Mommy. I'm still processing that unexpected sadness. I didn't think I wanted to be a parent, but I want to be involved with this kid. A role model they can trust with anything. Like my mom was to me and Jared is to Quent.

Quent rests in my lap for a while. I soak in the comfort of holding my sated lover close, shoring up my reserve of everything they mean to me. These fleeting moments are what I'll need to get through the next stage of this process. We're in a good place, our relationship is healthy. We can weather whatever comes our way. I believe in us enough to move ahead with what they want, even if it scares me.

My pup gets restless after a while. I suspect that's their human worries worming their way back in now that the scene is over. They squirm around, tipping up their face to look at me. I expect them to confess that they're worried. Scared of being pregnant. Instead, they ask about the logistics.

Classic avoidance that I should call out, but I'm afraid of what the future has in store for us too, so I go along with it. We might not be able to ignore the elephant between us forever, but for now, I want to savor the scene I just enjoyed with my pup. I want to bask in their excitement about the breeding scene I've got planned for them; the promise of a fantasy fulfilled.

"Are you going to have Doc inseminate me?" they ask, grinning at me. "I can't wait to do this for real. Thank you, Mommy."

"You're welcome, pup. We can include Doc. Or we can do it together at home with a stud pup. They even have toys designed for that purpose." That's something I know will thrill them to try.

"Like, with a knot?" Quent perks up at the possibility, as I expected, bouncing in my lap.

"Have you been reading more of those filthy shifter stories again, pup?" I squeeze their ass.

"Yes. Heat sex is a hot fantasy, Mommy." Quent presses back into my hands.

"Is that your fantasy, love? Do you want Mommy to breed you with a big fat silicone knot? Knock you up with a cute little baby for your brother?" I tease and Quent grinds our crotches together until I mention Jared.

"You had me all hot right up to mentioning Jar." Quent pulls a grossed out face.

I chuckle, because I knew that would cool even my insatiable pup's ardor. "Fair enough. We can go toy shopping. I've already got the pee tests our GP suggested for pinpointing when you're fertile and Logan is ready to provide the genetic material when we tell him it's time. You're really sure, love? We can do your breeding scene either way," I offer one last out. I'm not ashamed to admit that I hope they'll take it.

"Yeah, I really am. I'd rather avoid as much of the medical stuff as we can, so using my eggs is easier. And it kind of adds to the fantasy side of it. I know that's weird."

"It's not weird." I kiss their forehead. I don't mention that any pregnancy is going to require regular prenatal appointments. They know what they are getting into and they still want it. Besides, after years of dealing with crappy care, we switched to a GP who is trans-friendly, so that part won't be so bad. I already confirmed our doctor or someone from her practice can deliver the baby. Preying on their doubts isn't helpful if they are determined to walk this path. From here on out, my role is offering them nothing but support and love, no matter how much it hurts.

"Yeah, but like, I feel like it's kind of invalidating on some level to want to use my uterus." Quent drums their fingers along my shoulders.

"Do you think not having a womb makes me less of a woman?" I know the answer, and sure enough, Quent looks horrified at the suggestion.

"No!" They shake their head emphatically. "Of course not. I'd say that's not what I meant, but I guess it's the underlying assumption, huh?"

"A bit." I bop their nose gently.

"Okay. Well, that's bullshit. So I guess my brain is fixating on stupid shit. Sorry, Mommy."

I give them a squeeze. "You're allowed to have insecurities, pup. It's okay to be worried about how you'll respond to everything. I have concerns too, but you know that."

"Yeah. I'm hoping it won't be so bad. My mom was pretty much flat-chested even after nursing two kids, so I guess genetics are on my side there." Quent forces a laugh. "Part of me likes the idea of this marking me. And part of me fears it will fuck with my head."

Ah. Well, that answers some of my questions about why they are tying up their interest in surrogacy with kink. "You want it to be me marking you forever, pup?" The idea of me being the one to impregnate them makes my guts twist like I might puke. It's wrong for me on a visceral level. But from the perspective of leaving a permanent mark on them, I can understand where they're coming from. They love when I mark them. They fiddle with their collar at the mention of forever. I rest my fingers over theirs.

"Yeah. I love Jar. I want to help him grow his family. But you're the only one I want to have marking me, leaving an imprint on my body that I'll always carry, you know?"

My collar on their neck reassures us both. We can get through anything as long as we have each other. I truly believe that.

"Now you're talking like you want me to brand you." I tug on one of their ears playfully. Quent shudders.

"No, pain like that isn't my thing. And I don't want the marks for their own sake. It's the total package. Like this primal ownership thing? I don't know. I guess it's weird to talk about it like that because on an intellectual level, that's not how I think about sex. It makes me feel like a bad feminist."

"But as a sexual fantasy, it turns your crank?" I press.

"Pretty much." Quent shrugs self-deprecatingly, then clutches for the blanket when the movement causes it to slip off their shoulders.

I readjust the soft cotton more snugly around them. "You know it's okay to enjoy fantasies that would suck if they were real, right?"

"Yeah."

"So, I'm going to set this up for you. We can figure out how much you want to make the pregnancy a focal point of our play times as we go along. It's okay if you don't enjoy it as much as you think you will. And it's okay to love being my shameless little slut who loves being knocked up for their Mommy."

"You'll be okay with that?"

"Yeah. You getting knocked up *for* me is fine. I draw the line at being the one who breeds you. But I can push the plunger on the syringe while you pant over the stud of your dreams fucking you senseless, no problem. I like the idea of you desperate to be bred. Begging and needy, all because I want to watch him make you come undone on his knot. Is that what you want?"

"Yeah. And then I want you to sit on my face until your clit can't take anymore." Quent grinds against me.

I laugh at that. "That's my insatiable pup. Can't get enough of your Mommy, can you, baby?"

"Never."

"Mm. Are you ready to go home and show me just how much my puppy loves to eat pussy?"

"Yes, please." Quent scrambles up off my lap, all but tripping when they get tangled in the blanket. I catch them before they can fall, fold the blanket up, and guide Quent back to the locker room.

As I remove their puppy gear and pack it into our toy bag, I take my time touching and teasing them. I button a blouse over my lace accented corset top. They pull street clothes over their leather harness and we head home.

We still haven't touched on all the doubts we're both harboring, but I don't think sharing my fears now would change anything, other than to make them feel bad. We've said enough that I'm comfortable with the scene Quent wants. Quent is determined to do this, so we'll just have to see it through.

Besides, our doctor mentioned that it might take quite some time for them to conceive, so we should have plenty of opportunities to continue this conversation. And in the meantime, I plan on savoring every moment with my pup before everything changes.

Quent spends most of the drive home pawing at my thigh. Their fingers caress me, mostly sticking to the top of my leg, but every so often straying higher or dipping toward my inner thighs. They're pushing the limits of what I'll allow them to get away with when I'm driving, and we both know it. A sharp glance their way at a traffic light gets me an apology when their fingers brush too close to my clit.

They're off like a shot for the bedroom as soon as we get home. When we first agreed to try having an open relationship, I'd worried that Quent might not remain as invested in our sex life if they were sleeping with other people. That hasn't been the case at all. When I asked them about it, they kissed me and told me that sex was sex, but getting to make love with me was about more than orgasms. That hasn't changed over the years, but I still get a rush out of knowing how desirable I am in Quent's eyes.

They shed their clothing in record time. I clear my throat to get their attention. It only takes a pointed glance and an eyebrow raise to get them to put the discarded outfit into the hamper and put away their harness. I stow our gear bag in the closet to deal with later.

Quent flops naked onto our bed and gazes lovingly at me as I strip to my underwear. My lace panties match my corset. Quent licks their lips as I loosen the ties at the back and ease out of the undergarment.

"Come to bed?" Quent reaches toward me, like they want to stop me from taking it off yet. I know they're a fan of lace and the way the corset emphasizes my curves, but I've already worn the restrictive undergarment for hours since we left for the club. I really just want to let my boobs loose. It's got to go now that we're home.

"You want me, baby?" I slide the corset down over my hips and step out of it, aware of Quent's gaze drinking in my nakedness. I love the adoration in their eyes when they look at me.

"Yeah." Quent nods, shifting to sit on the edge of the mattress, legs spread wide. "I always want you."

"Mhm. And just what are you going to do with me?" I plant one knee on the mattress by their junk, pressing against them. I lean in close enough that if they shifted, we'd be kissing. Quent doesn't close the distance.

"I want to start with fondling your tits. Suck on your nipples until your clit is aching for me, pounding in time with your pulse. Then I want to lick you through those pretty panties and make you all sopping wet for me. Want to finger your pussy while I play with your clit until you're wild with lust. Want to make you so horny that you pin me down and use my mouth. Push your wet panties to the side and press yourself against my lips and tongue and ride my face until you're mindless with pleasure and panting my name." Quent's breathing gets heavier, hips lifting to grind against my knee by the end of their description. "Please, Mommy?"

"Yeah? What's my filthy pup get out of all that?" I press my knee more firmly into their groin, feeling their wetness as they grind against me. That's my insatiable love.

"I get to breathe you in. Taste your pleasure." Quent's eyes go unfocused as I reach down to rub my thumb over their junk, circling the sensitive head.

"Yeah? You enjoy tasting me, Quent?" I scrape my nail along their shaft, careful to give them just a hint of pain as they continue to hump against me.

"Ngh." They try to close their legs, clamping their thighs against my knee ineffectually. I give their junk a gentle squeeze. They stop trying to control the situation, relaxing and letting me take charge. I push them down onto their back, relishing the power exchange as they submit to me.

"Puppy, I asked you a question." I tweak one of their nipples. Quent arches into my touch.

"I love going down on you, Ky. I get to make love to you. Nothing's better than that."

Well, I can't argue with that sappy sentiment. And I know Quent means every word of it. Sweet words get sweet rewards, so

I lean over their body, kissing them until they are limp and pliant under me, their mouth open for me to plunder at will.

"Then make love to me, Quentin." I kiss them until the awkward position makes it uncomfortable. Then I scoot up the bed to straddle their hips. While I've got them pinned under me, I deepen the kiss.

Quent moans and tries to pull me down onto them. They like having my weight on them, but I don't want to dominate my pup tonight. Not that I don't love our dynamic, but sometimes I want to connect with Quent, my lover, and not just Q, my pup. I want to let my lover lavish their attention on me, the way they just described. I break our kiss and roll to the side. Quent whimpers plaintively when I move off of them. They lie on their back breathing heavily, turning their face to gaze at me.

"Ky?" they ask, seeking a command to follow. I can give them that, even as my name on their lips makes me shiver with want.

"Come get your treat, baby." I sweep a hand over my figure in invitation. Quent squirms closer to me and wastes no time in suiting actions to their earlier words, making love to me with their fingers and tongue for hours. They don't stop until we fall asleep tangled together under the blankets. Their devotion leaves me breathless and wishing we could stay like this forever.

CHAPTER 6

Quent

The thing about fantasizing over a one-off kink scene is that it's usually restricted to a steamy night at the club or in our playroom. What it isn't—under most circumstances—is lying still in our bed every morning for weeks while Mommy holds my thighs open to take my temperature. She also checks the fertility signs our doctor listed for us. It's not peeing into a little cup so she can use the test sticks we got for that.

Basically, finding out when we need to collect the semen sample from Logan isn't nearly as sexy as what I'd envisioned when I offered to be a surrogate. It's nothing like the dynamic Mommy and I share. This is intrusive and stressful.

None of this prep work is at all sexy. Granted, I prefer Mommy keeping track of all the fiddly details for me. If she hadn't taken charge of charting my fertile signs, I'd be tearing out my hair over the entire frustratingly slow process. I want to just skip to the good part and forget about the entire thing in the meantime. So I need her help with managing everything.

At first, Mommy tried to make it sexy when she was shoving the thermometer into me. That got old fast for both of us. So now she mostly pets my head. If I squirm, she tells me I'm a good pup and I just need to let her stick the pokey irritating thermometer in me for a little longer. Sometimes she kisses me to distract me while it takes roughly an eternity to get a reading.

I kind of like the excuse to just lay there in bed with her lips soft against mine.

The first couple of months after I went off T, Mommy's painstaking temperature charts didn't show much of anything. There was a bit of a spike for the week or so before I got my period back. But I figure today is more of the same when Mommy jots down her daily recordings without comment. As such, I get myself ready for work and leave without bothering to ask about the daily ovulation test result.

Work is the same usual grind dealing with customers. At least my bosses are cool. I left a more corporate chain for their independent pharmacy last fall and haven't regretted the change for a second. My last several jobs as a pharmacy tech were at big chains and I hated the corporate bureaucracy. Fran and Mikaela are kind of awesome though. They're a lesbian couple who own and operate the pharmacy and I like them and my other coworkers.

Alice, another of the techs, is even training me to be a mad scientist. Okay, it's not really mad science so much as compounding medications. I still get a kick out of making the pet meds we get orders for. When Alice was showing me all the weird flavor options, I almost cracked up laughing at those flavors. I still smile at the mental image of Mommy trying to use a medicine dropper to get beef shank flavored antibiotics down my throat next time I'm sick. I wouldn't put it past her to ask for the meat or peanut butter flavoring just to troll me.

During the day, I don't think much about the whole surrogacy or breeding thing. Well. Okay, there's a patient who needs Plan B, so that sort of makes me think about it. And a compounding order for a sick baby. I check the math on that one three extra times to make sure I get the dose right for our tiny little patient. And I have Alice check it too, before we hand it over to the pharmacist to triple check our work.

My last patient of the day comes up to the counter to ask for needles. They seem anxious about it, glancing around furtively, as though they expect me to grill them or deny them service.

"Oh, yeah, I hate when I accidentally get the wrong size. Why make it needlessly painful, right?" I make sympathetic noises to help them feel less self-conscious about their request. Even if it's not for a legal drug; better to have sterile needles than not.

"Yes!" A smile lights up their face at having an empathetic ear and they open up more. "That's what I said. The clinic gave us a larger gauge than the last cycle, and I'm enough of a grouchy walking disaster these days without having to inject through a freaking straw." The patient heaves a long-suffering sigh. "We're on our last injection cycle before we have to resort to IVF, so I'm over all the needles."

"I bet. Hope it works out this time. Let me grab the pharmacist to help you pick out the right size, ok?" I let Mik handle helping pick out what's needed. Then I ring up the equal parts anxious and hopeful looking customer. The whole encounter has me focused on what's going on with my body. Or more to the point, what isn't really going on yet.

I'm antsy over how little control I have over the entire process. I can't make myself ovulate or conceive or guarantee a healthy baby develops once I do. All I can do is hold my breath, figuratively, and wait for it to happen. And find as many fun ways to get my mind off it in the meantime as possible.

I know I'm being impatient. My doctor said it could take up to six months for things to get back to working order after my time on hormones. So I'm already ahead of the game. But now that it's all decided, I want to give Jared and Logan their baby yesterday.

I finish my shift all up in my head about it. That makes me quiet, which is not my usual. My toned down demeanor gets me concerned looks from my boss and coworkers, but I assure Mik

I'm fine and that I'll see everyone tomorrow. I head home with a squirmy sensation in the pit of my stomach that I need to *do something* to get my mind off all this interminable waiting.

I wish the club was open tonight and we could go blow off steam with a scene. Like something with Doc to get me out of my head. I text as much to Mommy from the parking lot before I start the car to head home.

Quent: Blargh. Weird day. I'm soooo restless. Puppy time tonight?

I don't expect a response right away. Mommy is usually working at this hour and not on her phone. So it surprises me when my cell buzzes with her reply as soon as I set it on the seat beside me.

Mommy: I've got you covered, Q. When you get home, I want you to take a nice long shower to decompress. Then come down to the playroom in the outfit I laid out on the bed. Two-legs on the stairs.

The news that she planned a scene for tonight has my libido raring to go. I love when she gives me vague hints about what we're doing. At this rate, I'm going to be restless and so hot and bothered I'll need to make that shower a cold one by the time I get home.

Mommy: Or, in other words, I already ordered a pizza.

Mommy throws in a quote from *The Room*, which makes me smile and takes some of the edge off my horniness. She has a thing for quoting it. Even though it's arguably the worst movie that I've ever sat through. She loves it. She likes weird stuff. But that's part of her charm. And I can't help quoting back at her.

Quent: Oh, Lisa, you think of everything! Or in other words, that movie is trash and you should be ashamed that you forced me to watch it.

Mommy: *The Room* is a cult classic, and no one tied you up or forced you to do anything. That time.

Quent: Are you going to tie me up and force me to do something tonight?

Mommy: Come home and find out ;)

Quent: You're tearing me apart, Lisa!

I can't resist one more of our favorite quotes as a parting line, but I wait a second for Mommy to reply before putting away my phone.

Mommy: LOL. You sure seem to remember a lot of that movie for someone who claims to hate it. Drive safe, Quentin. I love you.

Quent: No comment on the movie. :P Will do. Love you too.

Ky's right that I only pretend to dislike her favorite movie these days. It's grown on me over the years. I smile to myself at her use of the made up long-form of my name. Mommy is the only one who calls me that. It's not actually my name. But she does it when she wants me to know she's serious or shifting gears from silly and playful to Mommy-Domme mode. It means I better listen to her, or there will be consequences. And sometimes she uses it to emphasize that she sees and loves all of me. Even the bits I don't show most people.

I put away my phone and drive home. When I arrive, there's a car I don't recognize in our driveway. That's not super unusual. Mommy sometimes has clients come to her for consults. Especially if she knows them well. She does work for a lot of the folks in our social network. I try to shake off my irritation about a client horning in on my playtime. If Mommy said to meet her in the playroom after my shower, she'll have the client taken care of and out the door before it's an issue.

I might stomp up the stairs in a childish fit of pique at the intrusion regardless. Impulse control is not my strong suit. If she really is in her office working, I'll hear about my grumpy stomping later. That makes me feel a bit bad, so I walk more quietly down the hall to our room to take my shower.

I don't have it in me to subject myself to cold water when the warm spray pounds my back so wonderfully. Mommy didn't say I can't come. In fact, she said to decompress. So I take the edge off before soaping up with the relaxing lavender body wash Mommy must have dug out of the cabinet for me to use. Or she might have bought it for me? Either way, it smells nice and lathers up well. I'm in no rush with my ablutions. I don't hear anyone leaving, but over the sounds of the shower and the bathroom vent, it would be easy to miss, so that means nothing.

When I've wasted enough time that the hot water is no longer enticing, I get out and dry myself before padding to the bedroom. The outfit Mommy laid out for me is pretty simple. An unadorned harness made from narrow strips of dark leather that matches my collar, a headband with floppy pup ears attached, and a matching belted tail. She'll probably put on my paw pads and boots in the playroom because she doesn't like me wearing those on the stairs.

I put on the outfit, aware of my nudity and the vague possibility that Mommy might still have a client here. The naughtiness of the thought gives me a rush. There's no way she would have told me to wear this if it was someone who isn't part of the scene and in on whatever she has planned. Still, the anticipation is delicious as I skip down the stairs to find Mommy.

She's waiting for me in the playroom, like her message implied. But she isn't alone. The presence of two other people in our playroom makes any lingering annoyance at the strange car in our driveway evaporate. Not a work client who stayed late. Guests.

Guests who are here to play with us, judging from the full

hood on the pup currently humping into his handler's fist in the middle of the room. I recognize Niko and Clark, a married couple who are also into ENM from our regular puppy play group, but I only have eyes for Mommy.

As soon as I'm off the steps, I get on all fours and go to greet Mommy. Sure enough, she's got my paws all ready to go. She greets me by ruffling my hair and scratching behind my ears. I lick her face and wag my tail until she commands me to settle. Then I try to contain my enthusiasm and present each limb in turn for her to fasten on my mitts, knee pads, and boots.

"There, all ready." Mommy crouches in front of me and holds my head between her hands. "Who's my good pup?" she croons. I wriggle and try to lick her face, but she holds me back so I yip at her instead. "That's right, you are. My very good pup. And I have a surprise for you tonight."

She lets go of me and holds up a distinctive black bag.

I nose at the crinkly plastic, then paw at it, whining when that fails to reveal the contents. I look between Mommy and the bag and bark for her help. She chuckles and opens the top to pull out a large red dildo I recognize from my wishlist. It's got a thick knot at the base and a bit of tubing sticking out of it for fake cum. Or not so fake cum when the time comes.

The toy makes the penny drop. Tonight's the night. Excitement courses through my veins. This is it! I lunge forward to kiss all over Mommy's face. She laughs as she wraps her arms around my neck, partially to keep herself upright, judging from how much she leans on me. "I guess you like it, huh? Excited to have it inside you, Q?"

I voice my agreement with a louder bark and switch from licking her to nosing at the toy. The soft silicon is silky against my mouth and I can imagine how smoothly it will slide inside me. How the girth will stretch me. My orgasm in the shower isn't nearly enough to keep the rising tide of lust at bay. Tonight is going to be epic.

"You still want Mommy's stud to breed your tight little cunt?" Mommy asks, reaching between my legs to fondle me. "Is my little bitch in heat?"

I spread for her and whine when she just brushes her fingertips over my junk and rubs along the rim of my opening without giving me what I crave. She toys with me, touching without really stimulating me until I hump against her hand, trying to get her to touch where I want her. I whine in frustration, hoping she'll give me what I want.

"Horny little slut," she observes as she gently pinches my junk, squeezing just to the point of pain without crossing the line.

I whine louder.

"You can't wait to have this big, fat cock coming inside you, can you?" She flops the head of the toy against my cheek and I try to capture it between my lips, but she doesn't let me. "Show me you want it, pup."

I turn and present my ass to her, bowing down and spreading my knees so she has easy access to my bits, fore and aft. Mommy traces the dildo's cockhead over my T-dick to my hole, pressing it against the opening.

"It's going to fill you up with its seed, Q. Knock you up and make you all mine. You want that? You want to carry a litter of pups for me? Make your flat little belly swell for me? Give me nice round tits to play with? Show off how fertile my little bitch is for me?"

That, okay, in this context, it makes me moan and rock back on the toy she's holding at my entrance. But it also pulls me out of pupspace and makes my belly clench. It's jarring to hear her using words for anatomy I normally hate in reference to myself.

Most of the time, that would jangle around in my brain like

an alarm blaring out wrongness. Except I like it when it's about her owning me and using me, and that's probably weird. Right? It seems weird for those words to make me ache to be fucked, my arousal growing with every word. It's a conflict I don't want to explore right now. Not when I'm about to live out a fantasy.

I moan, as she sinks the head of the toy inside me and then pulls it back out, leaving me empty and clenching on air. "Mommy." I whine.

"You okay, baby?" Mommy asks. She pets my back between my shoulder blades.

"Yeah. Want it. Just. Weird."

"What's weird?"

"That I like the idea of that."

"What?"

"Tits and a belly."

"You said that's part of the appeal of the fantasy." Mommy has a cautious note in her tone, so I guess I might be worrying her with the break from pup mode.

I nod, not wanting to ruin the scene. I have considered this before. "Yeah. I thought it would be an acceptable tradeoff. Didn't think it would get me all hot."

"But it does?"

I nod. That's an understatement. Desire flows through my veins, molten hot.

"And that's freaking you out? Do you want to keep going or wait? We don't have to do it this cycle if you need more time to consider. Or did you want me to lay off the dirty talk?" Mommy offers. I ignore the hopeful note in her voice as she suggests postponing.

"No. I want to do it and I love when you talk to me like that. Just. Brains are weird. Um, does that mean the test showed I'm fertile today?"

"Yep."

"Neat."

Mommy chuckles and scratches behind my ears again. I lean into the touch and sigh in contentment, knowing she'll take care of me. I want to do this. The scene and the surrogacy arrangement. Mommy spends a bit more time petting and scratching me until I can sink back into my pup headspace again.

She doesn't let me have any more of my new toy until I'm whining for it. I end up on my back with her fingering me until I'm so close to coming I've all but forgotten the promise of a knot and cum inside me. Let alone the other pup in the room and his handler.

Mommy stops, giving me the command to stay. She whistles for Niko. So I stay on the floor on my back. I cock my head to see my friend attaching my new toy to a harness designed to accommodate him. His dick remains tucked inside a very snug-looking jock.

I want that pretty silicone dick inside me. Want it to breed me like Mommy promised. I shoot her a pleading look and she signals for me to wait. I whine. Clark, the other pup's handler, finishes with the straps, arranges the toy's tubing so that it will be accessible, and pats the other pup on the rump. Niko has his main focus on his handler, but he glances my way and whines.

"You want to mount the little bitch?" Clark suggests, sounding amused. The other pup barks an agreement. "That's good, because I agreed to let you knot them up tight and give them a pup. You ready to do that for me?"

The pup barks. I bark back. Mommy snorts. "Go on then," she

gives me the release command and I sidle toward the hired stud, presenting myself pretty much like an actual bitch in heat. He snuffles at my ass and licks all over my cunt and T-dick for a minute until I'm panting and whining for him to fucking mount me already. And then he does. His handler steps close to guide the dildo inside of me. Then the stud digs his front paws into my flanks, and fucks me hard and deep with the toy.

The textured shaft sends sparks of pleasure shooting through me, and I watch Mommy as she chats with the other handler and they both watch us impassively. Like she would if she brought me to a groomer. The stud breeding me is some sort of business transaction, and she's supervising services rendered and fuck if that doesn't have me all kinds of hot and bothered.

Plus, Niko feels really fucking good inside me. Plowing into me over and over, the glide of the dildo rubs me just right and drives me up to the edge. He's rough with me, and I know it won't stop when I come. That thought has my T-dick twitching with need. I whine and wriggle under him, seeking friction that Niko's paw mitts wouldn't let him give me, even if he cared to. Which he doesn't because he's just there to come inside me. He's here to breed me. I moan at that thought.

My wriggling seems to prompt the stud to shift gears. He stops thrusting in and out and presses the thick knot into me, stretching me impossibly wide. Looking at the dildo, I wasn't sure that bit would fit inside me, but as Niko patiently grinds against me, it works its way in. The gradual push mimics my fantasies of the slow swelling of a shifter's knot. The extra stretch tips me over the edge and my muscles spasm and clench around the toy. I let out a muffled moan that sounds more human than pup.

Mommy steps in close, and I catch her fitting a syringe to the tubing. Niko holds still, keeping the toy cock seated deep inside me as Mommy pushes the plunger. She reaches under me with her other hand to rub my belly.

"That's it, Q. Be a good pup and milk out every drop of his jizz. Let him knock you up, the way I know you want it."

I whimper as I grind back into the stud pup. Mommy slides her hand from my belly to my junk, rubbing the aching little erection there until I come again. The sensations peak and crash down over me. My entire world tilts on its axis at the waves of pleasure and the overwhelming realization that it's done. Mommy let him breed me. That makes me clench down harder.

My insides squeeze the soft silicone hard as I ride back into the guy it's attached to. I'm doing just what Mommy asked me to, being her good pup. It's one of the best orgasms I've had in a while. The pleasure seems to stretch into eternity as Mommy keeps her hand on me and the thick dick and knot stretch me wide. I imagine I could ride this wave of bliss forever and ever.

Of course it ends eventually. The stud pulls out, and I'm a wet and sticky mess. It's weird to think that this is the first time I've let anyone actually come inside me. Every other time it's been lube and my own fluids dribbling down my thighs after a good hard fuck.

Distantly, I'm aware of the other pup's handler removing the harness with the dildo still attached. Clark jerks Nicholas off while he begs his Daddy for it, just as shameless as I was for Niko to fuck me a minute ago.

Mommy urges me onto my back, fingers the dribbles that escaped back inside me, and slips a silicone period cup into place to keep the mess contained. We read on some fertility forums that other people doing at home insemination swear by them. And that practical little step brings reality crashing back down around me. We did it.

Mommy got a stud to breed me, just like I've fantasized about. He could've just knocked me up. Right now, there could be an egg just waiting to take up residence inside me for the next nine months. All my certainty that I can handle everything that entails seems laughable in this moment of insecurity.

"Mommy?" My voice is trembling as much as I am. It seems cold all of a sudden. Too cold. I shiver.

"I'm here. What do you need, Q?" Mommy drapes a soft blanket around me and lifts me into her lap. She fusses with my hair, gently removing my pup ears now that I am very much in my human headspace.

"You." I cling to her as the full weight of what I just did sinks in. I could find out I'm pregnant in a few short weeks. This could be it. My stomach roils at the thought. I don't know if I'm ready. I want to be, but it's a huge thing.

"You've got me. You've always got me. It's not too late to change your mind." Mommy soothes me.

I think of the patient who came in for Plan B. Her scared expression. I suppose I could take that. Might be too late to stop ovulation though. And I don't really want to. Just the thought has my protective instincts surging to the fore. I'd already do anything for the little ball of potential nibling cells that could, even now, be forming inside me.

Sure, all the unknowns leave me scared, but I still want to do this. I shake my head, my resolve hardening. "No. Not changing my mind. Just that was intense. I came so fucking hard, Mommy. You always take good care of me."

"Yeah? You sure it was Mommy and not the monster cock pounding your sexy little ass?" Mommy makes light of it. But I can tell she really would take me to get the medication if I wanted it.

"It's all you. You arranged it for me. Gave me just what I wanted. Watched me take the dick you picked out for me, just the way you arranged for it to happen. You gave me to him to breed, and I loved being yours like that."

"And did it live up to the fantasy?" Mommy plays with my hair. Her entire focus is on me, just the way I like it.

"More than." I smile at her.

"Good." Mommy kisses my forehead and wraps me tighter in the blanket. She rocks me from side to side as our guests wrap up their aftercare. Clark gets his pup some water and helps him to dress in street clothes when he seems steady enough to leave.

They both say their goodbyes to Mommy without disrupting my rest on her shoulder. I lift a hand in a vague farewell gesture, which makes Niko chuckle and shoot me a hand sign to call him later. Clark ushers him up the stairs. I'll have to thank him properly the next time we talk.

Mommy cuddles me until I stop shivering. Then she chivvies me into drinking some juice. I've long since stopped fighting against the local dominant types and their fixation on hydration after a scene. Whatever, the cool drink refreshes me as it slides down my throat, even if it makes me shiver again.

Mommy clucks her tongue at that. She wraps me up in her fuzziest bathrobe, and the warmth and the alluring scent of her favorite perfume lingering in the fabric warms me to my toes. By the time Mommy has fussed over and coddled me to her satisfaction, the immediate crash of nerves at the end of the scene is well past. We go up to our bed.

Mommy lets me fall asleep half on top of her. Some time later, I wake up when she kicks our blankets off the end of the bed, subconsciously seeking a reprieve from the additional body heat. I don't have the gumption to retrieve the blankets. Mommy is warm enough for me.

I snuggle even closer, her arms tighten around me reflexively. I wriggle to get comfy, awakening a dull ache from earlier. Mmm. That was a wonderful scene. I let my mind wander to how hot it was. The intense rush of emotions at being bred and fucked to my heart's content surpassed my fantasies. My fingers brush over my junk. I'm not planning on getting off really, just idly stroking while I relive last night's hotness.

And then my thoughts race right past the fun bits to the burning need to know if it worked. I know it's too soon to tell. Contrary to what I've read in my favorite shifter novels, it takes a few weeks to be sure. I hope it did. That I can soon present my brother and Logan with a baby to love.

There's also a tiny part of me that hopes it didn't. The part that wants an excuse for another scene like tonight. The part that isn't quite ready to go through with this. And I really just want to know either way. If I asked, I'm sure Mommy would arrange a repeat breeding scene for me regardless of whether there is any actual breeding happening.

I squirm, thinking of it and trying to sense any minute changes to my body until Mommy grumbles for me to sleep. I don't think she's fully awake. But I try to settle like her good pup.

It's hard though. I haven't been this restless since the night of my first T injection. I spent ages tossing and turning and trying to will the expected changes into existence.

The excitement caught me up, so that I set my expectations unrealistically high. Then it was a huge letdown that I had to wait for any noticeable changes. Despite knowing better, some wild part of me hoped I might find facial hair sprouting overnight. Or get instant bottom growth or a voice drop. All those things happened. Gradually.

Kylee's fingers scritch over my scalp, pressing my ear more firmly to her chest. My fidgeting woke her. Oops. I try to hold still and listen to the steady beat of her heart. The rhythmic thumps are soothing. A reminder that my love is here with me, come what may.

Peace settles over me. Mommy is here. I don't have to worry

about testing or the outcome of our first insemination attempt. Mommy will take care of it. The way she always takes care of me. I let the rise and fall of Kylee's chest under my cheek lull me back to sleep.

CHAPTER 7

Kylee

Quent left their breakfast dishes on the counter before work again. They finished the coffee without brewing a second pot too. So the lack of my usual morning caffeine doesn't make me more charitable about their uptick in scatterbrained behavior over the past almost two weeks.

I know it's been a wild couple of weeks. They're anxious about the surrogacy plan on top of finding out this week that Adventures has to close due to water damage. And just to add insult to injury, we lost our monthly puppy play venue to a scheduling conflict. So I've been trying to cut them extra slack and keep them distracted.

We also probably bit off more than we can chew by scheduling a huge play party for next week on short notice. The idea was to soften the news that our usual play spaces aren't available right now, but it's a lot to plan.

It doesn't help that my pup is a nosy little thing and not knowing the results of our insemination efforts is killing them. But the constant acting out is killing me. It's all minor stuff that adds up to something more going on with them. That's all the more reason for the party, a distraction from the test results, regardless of the outcome.

Stuff like forgetting their lunch in the fridge several times last week isn't unusual, but it's seemed amplified. They've also been falling into old habits that they know bother me. Like leaving their socks strewn across the den when they get home from work. I found their favorite chew toy stuffed between the couch cushions, along with the TV remote. I have rules about how they treat their chew toys for sanitary reasons, so breaking that rule is asking for a punishment.

And then there's the stuff they're doing out of a misguided desire not to bother me. They've been tossing and turning for half the night since our little breeding scene. I don't mind them waking me up to hold them when they can't calm their racing thoughts. It isn't a huge deal for me.

My work hours are flexible enough to allow me the occasional nap if I need it, unlike Q's job. But by the third night, they decided to correct the problem by not coming up to join me in bed for hours past their work night bedtime. That doesn't sit right with me.

It's like a confirmation of everything I've been worried about since they came home and told me they want to be a surrogate. This is already driving a wedge between us and I can't stand it. Waking to find them not in our bed hurts. No matter what else is going on, we've always prioritized our relationship, and them trying to hide their anxiety and nerves from me is like a slap in the face.

I've asked if they want to talk about it. With me or a third party. I'm hoping the play party we're hosting will help soften the impact of the test results by giving them something to look forward to. But so far, puppy time has done little to distract them from whatever is on their mind.

If I had to guess, it's the unknown. Are they pregnant or not? Q loves surprises, but they hate not knowing things. My nosy little pup must be on tenterhooks when the person they don't know something about is themselves.

I suggested inviting a friend over to play and take their

mind off it, since they can't seem to relax enough to get into their pupspace lately. But they just shrugged and said, 'maybe.' Despite their defiance of their work night bedtime, it was a relief to find them on the computer laughing over voice chat while they played a game with Connor last night. That was where I found them when I went down to check on them, since they still hadn't come to bed by midnight. Q seemed more themself as I listened in on the pair as they laughed and heckled each other.

None of the unusual behavior is enough to force Quent to talk when they aren't ready. But this latest minor rebellion with the coffee makes me want to put them over my knee to paddle their ass until they cry out all their fears. Then I can hold them while we talk it out and once their mood improves, I can kiss them breathless.

I love being the one who can make them come unglued. There's nothing like the rush of knowing my pup well enough that I can get in their head and make them face their emotions head-on. I get to be the anchor that makes it safe for them to let go of their fears and reservations. It's empowering.

When we do a scene, it's vulnerable beyond anything else. Nothing can compare to that heady rush. Not the thrill of finding a new favorite film, nor the satisfaction of finishing a challenging project, nor the fulfillment of organizing a successful event for our friends. I can't get enough of drinking in the raw openness they only give to me.

When Quent described why they were so keen on a breeding scene, how they want to give themself to me on a primal level, it painted a poignant picture. I understand the appeal now. From that perspective, of claiming them forever, I want that as much as they want to be mine in every way possible. It's another symbol of our love, like my collar around their neck.

The actual scene lived up to expectations. There was a moment when I thought I took it too far with the dirty talk, but then we paused to discuss. It was a relief for them to open up about their response to the scene so we could work through their reaction to the intense emotions together. I need that openness from them on every step of this journey we're taking.

That was what made me comfortable enough to move ahead. The proof that they would share their innermost thoughts and feelings with me. It made me feel connected to them in that moment in a way I wish I could recapture right now. That night, it was as though we were on the same page, connected on a deeper level by our mutual trust and love.

Now, I want to know what's going on in their heart and their head as they are clearly floundering. But I can't make them open up to me. Out of all the things I am and do, the most important to me is being Quent's Mommy and partner. I've always found that role empowering.

It's no wonder, considering that the strongest woman I've ever known is my mother. She fought for her place in the workforce. Stood up for me to be myself, even when she didn't understand me. Supported me when I finally had the courage to tell her who I am. Fought against the illness that claimed her far too young. She showed me how to be a strong woman before I realized or was ready to admit to myself—let alone anyone else—that I was one.

There's nothing more meaningful to me than being Quent's Mommy. And a tiny part of me wonders what it would be like to have a child call me that too. Quent and I agreed ages ago that we didn't want kids. I haven't regretted that choice in our years together. But a part of me is dreading what's ahead of us if they are pregnant. Will I be able to let go of a child they had a part in creating?

Part of me worries I won't. That I'm not strong enough to get us both through the next, however long it takes for them to give their brother the baby he so desperately wants. A selfish part of me wants the test to be negative and for Quent to give up on this scheme, but that isn't my choice to make. They're mine in every way that matters, but they're still their own person.

A spanking tonight might be the perfect reminder for us both that Quent is mine to nurture and care for. A way to show them I'm still in control, even when I doubt my strength. Realistically, I doubt they're going to act less scattered until we have an answer about their potential pregnancy though. Which is why I'm thinking I might not stick as strictly to the pregnancy test's included directions as I otherwise might.

Well, the coffee won't make itself, so I dump the used grounds, rinse and refill the reusable filter in the basket with fresh coffee, and brew another pot. Then I dump the crumbs from Q's plate into the food waste bin and wash the dish while my coffee percolates. I drop a bagel in the toaster and open the calendar app on my phone to my shared calendar with Q so I can change test day to tomorrow.

The box says to wait until after a missed period, but a lot of the fertility forums we've been reading through suggest you can get a positive sooner. It's been eleven days since the test said they were ovulating, so I figure it can't hurt to test at this point.

Their temperature chart is looking good, but that's not exactly diagnostic. I'm just hoping they aren't having second thoughts about the entire endeavor. And wishing I could trust that they'd tell me if they were.

I text for them to check the calendar when they get a chance. Then I check to be sure they remembered their lunch when I grab the cream cheese from the fridge. Their lunchbox isn't in there, so that usually means they remembered to bring it with them. Good. I have a redesign that needs to be done by Friday and ferrying lunches to them has eaten into my work hours lately.

I get a text back from Q as I'm settling in at my work desk

with my breakfast. They must have just arrived at the pharmacy if they are messaging me. Good timing.

Quent: Oh, thank god. I hate waiting.

They respond to the updated calendar without preamble, and that makes me smile. Leave it to Q to cut right to the chase.

Mommy: I know.

Quent: Sorry about the coffee. I didn't realize I forgot to make another pot for you until I was turning into the parking lot. I've been distracted.

Mommy: I know that too. I'm not mad. Just frustrated you've been keeping it all bottled in.

Quent: Yeah. I'm just trying not to dwell on wondering.

Mommy: Promise to tell me if you have second thoughts?

Quent: *eye-roll* I already promised that. I don't break my promises to you, Mommy.

Mommy: You've been acting off. And if I didn't know you had a lot on your mind, you'd have earned yourself a punishment several times over with all the messes you've left around the house.

Quent: I know. I'll try to pay more attention. It's a lot to wrap my head around, I guess. Like, it's sort of weird that I might be pregnant by Logan. Like ew? But also, it's not my kid. If there even is a kid. And because it's sort of weird to not know if it worked. And because I kind of want to do another scene like that. So I'm guilty that part of me wants the test to be negative so we can try again. And knowing we can't go to the club makes me really want to go.

Their candor makes me laugh.

Mommy: If you loved it that much, we can do it again either way. I promise that was not the only time you'll get to play with that toy.

Quent: Yeah, but without the actual jizz, right? I mean, if I am.

Mommy: If you like the texture of it, I can get some cum lube to shoot out of it next time.

Quent: Yes, please. And we can have another playdate with Niko?

Mommy: Of course. Anything else?

Quent: Nope. Unless you want to give me a spanking tonight? I've been a very naughty pup ;)

Mommy: You certainly have. I'll have to think of a suitable punishment. If you're up for that tonight.

Quent: More than. It helps to get my mind off it. Anyway, got to head inside to clock in now. Thanks for listening though. I love you, Ky.

Mommy: Love you too, Quentin. See you after work.

I send Quent a puppy GIF to make them smile, and then I tackle my work so I'll be free to keep them busy when they get home tonight. Parts of my current project require my full attention. But some parts I can do practically by rote.

Bug testing the links on the site I'm working on lets me mull over exactly what I'm going to do to my pup tonight. They need a reminder that there are consequences to breaking the rules. We both need the comfort of our roles.

I think they might still need a spanking. But first I'm going to make them clean the upstairs while they're wearing chastity with a vibrating plug I control stuffed inside of them. That ought to keep their mind occupied. It certainly has me distracted with fantasies of my sexy pup squirming for me as I finish up my work for the day.

CHAPTER 8

Quent

Test day. The thought registers as I wake up before my alarm. I stretch out under the covers, wishing I could go back to sleep, but knowing that ship has sailed. Even after the scene Mommy set up for me last night, I slept fitfully, worrying over the results.

It's no surprise that I woke up as soon as the first rays of dawn infiltrated our room, even though my alarm isn't set to go off for another hour. It's been ages since I woke up worried about a test. Not since school.

"Are you ready?" Mommy asks.

"Huh?" I tip my head to look at her.

She smiles as she rests a calming hand on my bouncing knee, drawing my attention to the motion. Oops. Guess I'm still fidgety, even after the very thorough punishment Mommy gave me last night. I wiggle to reignite the lingering ache in my ass and thighs.

"For the test. You might as well get up and do it. There'll be no living with you until you know."

"It's still early though. So even if it's negative, it might not mean anything." I wish I had my chewie to keep me occupied and my thoughts off the test.

"That's possible. Most of what I've read says it should show up by now though. Either way, you won't know until we do the test. Are you ready?" Mommy pats my thigh encouragingly.

"Yeah. Come with me?" I twine our fingers together.

"Of course." She raises my hand to her lips and kisses me.

We get up. Once we're in the washroom, Mommy reads off the test instructions for me, handing me the unwrapped test stick. I follow her directions, put the cap over the peed on part of the test, and wash my hands. Then I sit on the toilet lid to stare at the test field. The control line fills in, bright pink right away.

"Is it negative?" I ask, holding it toward Mommy.

"Be patient, pup. The instructions say you should wait three minutes to read the results."

"Yeah, but the control line is there already. So it worked, right? And there's...huh, okay, there might be a faint *something* now?" I point at the thin line that caught my eye as I waved the stick toward Mommy. She takes it from me and sets it on the counter.

"I set a timer. We'll look for a line when it goes off. In the meantime, why don't you brush your teeth?"

I huff and grumble, but I do as she said, knowing that it's one hundred percent a distraction technique. It works well enough. Except I keep stealing glances at the test stick. And there's definitely something there now, right? I think? When I look at a certain angle. Mommy covers the test with a square of toilet paper.

That initial blank white field made me really want this. It's like every nerve in my body is super sensitized and I'm vibrating with anticipation. I want to call Jar and Logan and tell them they're going to be daddies. Now that the potential for it is so close, I want that more than I thought I would, with a deep longing that's an almost physical ache.

I want to have a nibling to spoil. I want to give them that. The chance to take all the unused baby gear out of the hall closet where they shoved the physical reminders of their grief and fill their home with joy again.

And I want it for myself too. In my mind's eye, I can already picture fun babysitting outings with Mommy, me, and this baby. Family game nights with Jared, Logan, and their kids gathered around the table. I don't want to be a parent, but I want to be a part of this baby's life. I want them to exist with a greedy need.

"Spit." Mommy interrupts my thoughts with a reminder to finish brushing as her phone timer beeps. I comply, rinsing and putting away my toothbrush before turning to where she's holding the test.

"Well?" I make grabby hands and she turns it toward me. Two lines. The second one isn't anywhere near as dark as the control, but it's there. Positive. "Whoa."

I sit hard on the toilet again as the enormity of the answer hits me like a ball to the face. I'm really doing this. This is what I wanted, so why does it hit me like a gut punch, like the wind got knocked out of my lungs and I can't breathe?

"Oh, wow. We're really doing this," I say it out loud, because that's pretty much all I can process right now. The hypothetical has become real, and this is happening.

"Quentin?" Mommy watches me intently, but I didn't catch whatever she was asking.

"Wow." I meet her eyes and swallow hard, fingers going to my collar in a self-soothing gesture as panic swells up inside me, making my breathing and pulse speed. "That, uh, happened faster than I expected."

I don't think I'm ready to handle this. And of all the absurd thoughts to zoom in on, the one that sticks in my head is that I'm going to start showing while it's still warm weather. I won't be able to hide my bump under baggy clothes. How soon is that going to be an issue?

Oddly, instead of fear, thinking about this kid growing inside me sparks the joy I expected to suffuse me at the news. I'm going to have a big fat baby bump because there's going to be a new baby in our family. One I get to dote on and love and hand over to their parents at the end of a visit.

My emotions spin like a kaleidoscope, shifting patterns that shatter and reform before I can really hone in on them. The panic recedes as I focus on the vision of a future where I get to hold my nibling in my arms someday soon. That's what I want. And I can get through the next nine months to achieve that goal.

"Color?" Mommy asks when my answer to her question doesn't allay her concerns.

"Green. Very green. Just processing." I don't think to ask her the same; Mommy is always a rock for me when I need her.

"Take as much time as you need." She rubs my back and I lean into her hand.

Mommy's comforting presence makes it easier to lean into the excitement. It worked, and now there's a set timeline on this process. I smile as I finger my collar, happiness suffusing me. That's the part I want to focus on, not the doubts and fears.

"Yeah. Um, can we go visit Jar and Logan to tell them in person?" I pull my fingers away from the collar with an effort.

Telling them means I can't pretend it didn't work if I change my mind. I don't want to change my mind, but I'm afraid I might if I let myself think about it all too hard.

"We can," Mommy says. "Do you want to tell them today?"

"Yeah. Yes. Now? Can we go now?" I glance out the window where the sun is still barely peeking above the horizon. "Or is it too early?"

Mommy snorts. She doesn't stop rubbing my back. "I somehow think this is the sort of news they wouldn't mind waking them, but how about we pick up coffee for them on the way to celebrate?"

She's suggesting that to give me more time to change my mind. I wrinkle my nose. "I told them I'd cut back to one cup a day while I'm—" As the word trips out of my mouth, it really sinks in that I'm pregnant. "—pregnant." That isn't nearly as exciting as thinking about a fully formed, living, breathing baby at the end of the road. I don't want to *be* pregnant. What I want is to have already done this. Fuck, there goes my chill. "I'm pregnant," I repeat.

"Yeah." Mommy nods.

"What if it's awful?" I try to shove down the panic that's back clawing at my throat. It's going to be fine. Everything has to be fine. I can ignore it for a while. It's not like anything will be really noticeable for several months yet.

"Then you have options."

I shake my head. "Nope, I'm not taking this away from them again. I can handle it." Telling them now means I'll have to. I refuse to hurt them again. The sooner I tell them, the better.

Mommy sighs. "Then I guess, if it's awful, it's an awful thing you did because you love your family."

I nod. "Yeah." I take a deep breath to settle my thoughts. "Okay, well, if I'm only allowed one coffee a day, I'm making the most of it; can we go to Sin and Chocolate?"

"Of course. Get ready and we'll swing through downtown before we head over to their place to give them the news. Are you sure you're green about this?"

"Yeah. I mean, I'm nervous about it, but I'm mostly happy. This kid is going to be so loved, Mommy."

"Yeah, they will." She pulls me into a hug, stroking my hair and pressing a kiss to my forehead. "Our entire family will adore them."

"I can't wait to meet them." I leave unsaid that part of my excitement is the desire to put the hard parts behind me. Mommy will understand that. I bounce on my toes to kiss her cheek.

"You will, soon enough, and we'll keep you plenty busy while you have to wait. Now, scoot. If you want time to tell your brother before your work shift, we need to get the show on the road."

***

Logan answers the door when we get to my brother's place. He's half-dressed for work, in suit pants and an undershirt, and he has his body angled toward the kitchen, so he can continue his conversation with Jared.

At first, when he opens the door, he looks puzzled. Like he has no idea who would visit this early. That morphs to surprise at seeing Mommy and me with a tray of fancy coffees. Mommy has her arm around me, supporting me, but letting me guide the interaction. She gives me the strength to stand there smiling about the news that's still sinking in for me.

"Good morning, lovelies," he greets us warmly. Then a huge smile blooms on his lips. His eyes dart from my face to my belly and then back to my face with an unasked question in his gaze.

"Babe, your sibling is here," Logan calls back over his shoulder. Jared comes into the hallway, and I can tell they're both trying not to hope too hard. It makes me glad I have the good news they're obviously afraid to ask about.

"Hey, Quent, to what do we owe the pleasure?" Jared asks, one arm wrapped around his husband's waist, mirroring the way

Mommy is holding me.

Logan holds my brother's hand, the two of them bracing themselves for my answer. As if I'd come over here and get their hopes up with no warning if the news wasn't good.

Seeing him full of hope settles something inside me. I can do this for him. Not just can; I want to. I'm so excited to see him be a dad. My earlier joy is back, blocking out my nerves as it bubbles through me along with all the dreams of the future I have for him and this kid.

I can't hold in my excitement for them. I glance up at Mommy and she smiles her encouragement at me. Her support makes me bold enough to dive and commit fully here. I step toward my brother.

"Rude, Jar, you're just going to leave a pregnant person standing on the front steps?" I tease, shoving the tray of coffees toward my brother-in-law. I wasn't sure how I wanted to word it, but they have to know that's why I'm here. To tell them in person. And I'd rather celebrate inside than in front of the house.

"You are?" Jared asks, still wary of believing this is real.

"It worked?" Logan asks.

Neither of them takes the tray of coffees. Instead, they both gawp at me like I'm a mythical imaginary creature who's come to life on their doorstep to offer them their heart's desire. Well, I guess that last part is exactly what I'm doing.

"It worked; you two are going to be dads!" I announce. "Duh, as if I'd come here before work to ruin your day with bad news."

"That's amazing," Jared exclaims, his eyes lighting up with joy, just the way I'd imagined this moment.

"Thank you!" Logan says. And the two of them embrace.

Logan and Jared exchange one of those besotted couple looks, and then Logan kisses my brother. Mommy loops her arms around me while we wait out their celebratory embrace. Their eyes lock and I swear they have an entire conversation in those seconds of eye contact, and then they both step aside and invite Mommy and me inside.

"Want to come in and have that coffee with us?" Jared asks, gesturing toward the kitchen with a beaming grin firmly in place.

"Yes, please. I know you two have to get to work, and so do I, but I wanted to tell you in person," I say. "I hope that's okay?"

"More than okay, you're always welcome to visit anytime, Q," Logan assures me.

"I know. You guys love me; it's in the sibling contract Jar signed," I tease them as I set the travel tray of coffees on the counter. There's no sibling contract, but I like to tease the two of them since they're both lawyers. Though I did sign papers with them about this kid.

Jar assures me it's an agreement and not a contract. And Mommy went over it with her lawyer to be sure the terms take care of me. Which they do. My brother wouldn't pull anything shady with me. It's just a really wordy document saying he and Logan agree to pay for all my pregnancy related needs. And I agree to sign away all the parental rights I never wanted for this kid.

I already know from the short time Thomas was in their home that they'll let me be a huge part of the kid's life. From the hungry way Mommy has been looking at my belly since we got the test results, I suspect she's going to be a doting aunty too. We might have to talk about the kid thing again after this. I still don't want to be a parent. I hope this doesn't change her opinion about that.

"Wow. I can't believe it worked on the first attempt." Jared sounds dazed. "You have no idea how much this means to us, Quent." And then my brother hugs me. It starts out as a bear hug, his arms wrapped around me tight, reminding me of being his kid sibling back when he was my home.

I cling to him, so *so* happy to finally repay some tiny fraction of what he's done for me over the years. And then he softens his hold, like I'm delicate and breakable and I don't like that at all. It makes me bristle, muscles tense, skin prickling. Anger that this is already changing the perception of who I am is a flash of searing heat inside me, there and gone.

"Thank you so much, Q," he breathes the words into my ear, and even in a whisper, his voice almost breaks with emotion.

That quells my irritation. He still won't get away with treating me like I'm made of glass for the next nine-ish months, but today he gets a free pass. I hug him back for a long moment.

Then Logan claims me for a hug too, and I have a weird moment thinking about him and how there's some genetic piece of him floating around inside me right now. It makes my head spin. Trippy. I shove the thought away. It's my nibling, not a glob of Logan's DNA. That's easier. I can have warm fuzzy thoughts about that.

I give Logan another squeeze, and then I fall on the coffees. Drink distribution is a valid distraction to keep me from dwelling on that moment of weirdness. As I make sure everyone gets their morning caffeine, I babble about the next steps and Jared and Logan ask questions as needed.

Jared's eyes keep darting to my midsection, and it makes me self-conscious. I take a seat at their kitchen table, leaning my elbows on it to hide my nonexistent baby bump. I sip my coffee. Mommy sits beside me and rubs my back comfortingly. Her unwavering support grants me the strength to do anything. I cast her a side-long smile that she returns.

"So, yeah. I want you two involved with the pregnancy as much as you want to be. I mean. Within reason. Like. I'll stick by what we agreed to, but I don't need you checking up on my caffeine levels and dietary stuff."

"Sure. We wouldn't dream of getting between you and your cheese fries, sib," Jared teases. "Pregnancy cravings are no joke. Or so I've heard. Just let us know when and where to be, and we'll be there." He turns to lean against the counter, facing Mommy and me with his coffee.

I grin at the reminder and glance at Mommy. "Oh, yes, the cravings. The internet says they can start super early."

"Does the baby suddenly want cheesy fries, Quentin?" Mommy teases me. She's totally on to my plan to milk that for all it's worth. But I don't think she'll call me on it, if I don't abuse the privilege too terribly. Her eyes sparkle. Warm pools I could dive into and lose myself in if we were alone.

"Want an omelet?" Logan offers. He already has a bunch of ingredients prepped on the counter, but I catch the way he and Jared keep giving each other moony-eyes. "Wouldn't want to send you to work hangry." He and Jared are standing close, and I know they're dying for privacy.

We should go, no matter how good Logan's omelets sound right now. Jared is flashing Logan one of those speaking couple looks. This one is saying something along the lines of *'what are you doing? Don't we want them to leave so we can bang?'* I hold back a snort at his ill-concealed frustration. Logan rubs his husband's shoulders. Jared turns to face him and they just smile the sappiest smiles I've ever seen at each other. Happiness radiates off them both.

Their joy makes me all kinds of proud to have given them the hope they've been lacking lately. I haven't seen them smile this much in ages. Not since their brief time with Thomas. This is why I'm forging ahead with being their surrogate, despite all my looming fears. I want them to have this.

I grope for Mommy's hand. Her touch is the reminder I need that I have that same forever love they share to get me through the struggles inherent to giving them everything they want. Mommy takes my hand and squeezes. When I turn to face her, she tips her head toward the door, indicating that we should go.

I know she's right that Jared and Logan need alone time now, time I have no problem giving them. Except I also kind of enjoy torturing them by lingering. As much as I love them both, it's still my duty as a little sibling to cockblock big bro. For old times' sake.

"Hm, that does sound good," I muse. "And since I'm making you guys eggs, too, fair is fair."

Mommy flashes me a warning look that tells me she knows exactly what I'm up to. I got a cookie bar from the cafe so she knows I've already eaten. She lets me have my fun for now though.

Jared makes an exaggerated grossed out face and I stick my tongue out at him. "Ew, that is not how I'd phrase that. You're charming as ever, Quent."

"Hm, guess I must've been raised in a barn or something." I shoot back at him. Lately he's been too sad for this type of cheery banter, and I'm so relieved to have this part of him back that his ribbing only makes me grin.

"Did you really want an omelet?" Jared asks with a reluctant sigh. His eyes narrow at me with that parental look that says he sees through my bullshit.

"Not really, no. We got pastries on the way here," I admit, smirking at him. "Just busting your balls."

"That's what I thought. Get out of here, you brat." Jared shoos me away. "I hope your mommy spanks you for teasing us."

"Hey, it's fine. I don't mind cooking," Logan says.

"Yeah, and it's sweet of you to offer, but I have to get to work, and we should give you two privacy." I smile at them, hopping up from my chair.

"Seriously, go to work, Q." Jar grabs a dish towel to flap it at me. I blow a raspberry at him. Then I pull him into a hug, glad to have my playful brother back.

"I love you. I'm really excited to meet this little critter and hand them over to you guys. Go celebrate with your boo." As I say it, I can already picture how saccharine sweet and gooey he's going to be as a dad. Wrapped around the kid's little finger. I can't wait until that day. Not just because it will mean I'm no longer pregnant, either. I'm excited to meet the kid and watch my brother and Logan fall in love with their child.

Jared squeezes me tight this time, not treating me with kid gloves like earlier, to my immense relief. "Thank you, Q. Seriously. You didn't have to do this for us," he murmurs near my ear.

"I want to do it." I shrug off his effusive thanks. "So, I'll text with the deets about appointments later."

I hug my brother-in-law, too, and then I head for the door. Mommy says her goodbyes and follows me. I glance back to see my brother holding Logan in the hallway, kissing his neck as they move toward their bedroom. Yeah, definitely time to leave them to it. I throw a wave over my shoulder and shut their front door.

"How are you doing, pup?" Mommy slings an arm around my shoulders, pulling me in to kiss my temple before she guides me back toward our car.

"Good. Did you see how happy they were?" I ask, eager to share my joy with her.

"I did." She smiles indulgently at me. "And I saw your little game at the end there too."

"That was nothing. I was such a little shit when they started dating. Did I ever tell you how I used to make it difficult for them to have alone time?"

"You've mentioned it a time or two." Mommy sounds amused as she helps me into my seat, does up my seatbelt for me, and gives me another quick kiss.

"Yeah." The conversation pauses as she goes around to the driver's side, but I resume talking once she's buckled in. "I'm lucky Jar's got the patience of a saint and Logan understood I was acting out of insecurity that I'd lose Jar to him. He wasn't the first boyfriend I made a sport of cockblocking, just the first to stick around and win me over."

"He charmed you with his cooking, right?" Mommy asks as she pulls into traffic.

"Yeah. Pretty much. And he's perfect for Jared. Anyway, drop me off at work? I'll bus it home tonight, so you don't have to worry about picking me up later."

"That would be ideal. I've got deadlines closing in on me. And a few more party details to arrange, mostly chasing down RSVPs so we know how many to expect, or I'd be happy to give you a ride both ways."

"It's fine. Want to celebrate getting me knocked up later?"

"Did you have anything particular in mind?"

"Cheese fries?" I suggest hopefully.

"You are incorrigible. I'll put in an order for your favorite appetizers and then you can earn them when you get home."

"Oh. Yes, please. How?"

"That's for Mommy to know and you to find out later."

I squirm in my seat at the delicious anticipation. The dull ache from last night's spanking has already faded completely. That works for me. Whatever she wants from me, knowing I'm going to have to perform for her tonight has my libido revving already.

"I'm going to be horny all day, wondering what we're doing tonight." I whine, tugging the loop on my collar.

Mommy pats my thigh with zero sympathy. "Seems fair, considering you were trying to make Jared and Logan too late for work to have time to celebrate their good news properly."

"Yeah, but that's different." I squirm in my seat, uncomfortably full after my pastries. Or maybe a bit bloated. Is that a pregnancy thing?

"How?" Mommy shoots me a no-nonsense glance that says she isn't buying what I'm selling.

"Because I lack impulse control?" I tug at my seatbelt.

"And this is an excellent reminder of why it's important to work on having patience." She rests her hand on my thigh to settle me. It works. Mostly. I stop squirming.

"I have loads of patients. At work. Pretty sure they want their prizes right this second too." I pout.

"Prizes, huh?"

"Meds, prizes, same thing."

Mommy chuckles. I love her laugh, and that I can make her sound so happy. That's always been something I treasure.

"Sure thing, antsy pants. Why don't you take advantage of the drive time to call about that appointment? And don't forget to get your prescription updated. Our doctor said you need to increase your levothyroxine once you get knocked up," Mommy reminds me.

I grumble about it, but it's a good idea. Having something external to focus on is usually helpful, so I make a first prenatal appointment. My doctor also confirms that I need to do blood work ASAP to check how my microscopic nibling is already impacting my thyroid levels. So she's faxing paperwork to the pharmacy for me.

Good thing my employers are super chill and already know all about my surrogacy plans. It's always weird to me that healthcare is so reliant on archaic technology like fax machines. Today that will make things more convenient for me.

The passing scenery and the constant hum of the car engine lull me into closing my eyes to rest after I text my brother and Logan the deets about my appointment. I'm sleepy from waking up early. And probably being preggers. And my thyroid. Ugh, I hope the next several months aren't as exhausting as my thyroid issues before I got them diagnosed.

The constant fatigue was the worst. I wanted to get up and do things, but my mind was all fuzzy, my body heavy as lead, and I was always cold. My periods were like Niagara Falls, which put me in an even worse depression spiral than usual during shark week.

Okay, so, all of it was the worst. Or it might have been the not knowing why I felt so terrible all the time that was the worst. There were lots of worst parts, to be honest. This isn't that bad. Yet. I yawn, wishing there was time for a nap before my shift. There isn't and dozing off in the car will only make me more groggy. I squirm around to shake off the sleepies.

I consider texting Connor, but then Mommy pulls up at the pharmacy. On second thought, I'd rather give my best friend the news in person. I yawn as I get out of the car and Mommy has to call me back to get the lunch I forgot out of the back seat.

"Take it easy today, pup; you look exhausted." She takes hold of both my shoulders and plants a kiss on my forehead. I lean into her for a long moment, breathing her in for as long as she'll hold me.

"Didn't sleep well last night," I say through a yawn. "Too excited about the test."

"Good thing today is your Friday, huh? You can sleep in tomorrow." Mommy rubs my back comfortingly. "Still want me to plan some play for tonight?"

"Yeah. And cheesy fries." I nod enthusiastically.

That makes her laugh. Mommy ruffles my hair the way she plays with my ears when I'm in pup mode and I lean into the touch. "You'll be late for your shift, pup. Get in there." She sends me on my way with a gentle swat on my ass and I go.

At least my bosses are understanding. Fran is the opening pharmacist today. She arches a brow at me as I walk in five minutes late. I'm still pulling my short lab coat over my scrubs.

"You look like hot garbage this morning. Anything we should know?" Fran is holding up my new prescription, along with the prenatal lab requisition forms I had my doctor fax over.

"Bite your tongue, I'm *glowing*." I tease as I take the papers from her and get my work area arranged.

"So, you're pregnant?" Fran says dryly as she pulls the next prescription to check toward her.

"Yep. I'm knocked up with my brother's baby; it's some real daytime television shit," I joke.

Hans, a student intern who hasn't been around long, does a spit take. "You what now?" He looks a little green at the thought. Okay, so yeah, that probably sounded worse than I intended. I don't know his story, so maybe not the most sensitive joke. At least there aren't any customers in the area yet.

Alice cracks up laughing though. She's been dealing with my grumpy ass complaining about having to stop my T and cut back on my coffee intake over the past few months. Al keeps reminding me it will be worth it to make this nibling happen. She gets me. We exchange a smile.

"I'm his surrogate," I explain, since Hans looks like I broke his brain. "Jared and his husband are going to be the best dads."

Our intern relaxes, giving me a tentative smile. I don't know the kid well, but Fran and her wife aren't at all shy about being openly queer. Alice talks about her girlfriend all the time too. And none of my coworkers batted an eye when I slipped and called Ky Mommy in the break room. So I know it's okay to talk about Jar and Logan here.

"Oh, that's, uh, real nice of you, then." The kid looks like he means it, even if he finds pregnancy talk awkward.

"It's not entirely altruistic; I want a nibling to spoil." I shrug. "So, I guess I need to up my levothyroxine?"

"Yep, you should just need a few extra doses per week for now. Want to use up what you have at home and I'll put the new instructions and amount on file so you can get an earlier refill when you run out?" Fran offers.

"Yeah, the doctor gave Ky the instructions when we saw her, so I'm sure she'll be all over making sure I take the right amount."

"Perfect. Now, why don't you work on making blister packs for the LTC facilities today, since you look dead on your feet?" Fran suggests in a tone that brooks no argument. She doesn't want me screwing up on filling prescriptions, which is fair enough.

Pre-filling blister packs for the long-term care facilities that the pharmacy services is monotonous. The scanner we use on the barcodes makes it hard to screw up what goes where. Plus, it's going to get double checked at least twice before it even leaves the door. Basically, it's a foolproof way to minimize any potential for errors while I'm not at my best.

"Sounds good," I agree, and move to the designated area to get to work. Fran's efficient handling of accommodating my needs today eases some of my tensions about this entire thing. The people I spend the most time around are all supportive.

It's too bad I spend the entire morning yawning and I'm too queasy to eat more than a few bites at lunch. I thought I'd have more time before this pregnancy made itself known. And that makes me worry that something is wrong.

I ping-pong between being excited about the pregnancy and nervous that the symptoms are only going to get more intense as this progresses. And I wish I could just go home and curl up with Mommy while I try to sort through my reactions. It seems like I'm all over the place emotionally when I just want to be excited for the new addition to our family.

CHAPTER 9

Kylee

I meant it when I told Quent I was too busy to pick them up after work today. But the way they dragged their feet when I dropped them off changed my mind. I don't want my pup riding the bus when they're the next thing to sleepwalking. So I rearrange my schedule and bring my laptop with me. It's an empty promise to myself to squeeze in some work while I wait for their shift to end, since I arrive a little early. Better that than risk missing them.

I don't end up getting much work done. As much as they were struggling to process the news, I'm having a hard time getting my head around it too. I was certain that at the very least, this would take multiple attempts. That we'd have more time to prepare mentally. But it happened fast and now my Quent, the love of my life, is pregnant with a child we aren't keeping.

Much as I appreciate the close bond between Q and their brother, that's still hard to accept. It's like a loss of something I don't even have. Dread, aching and raw, simmers inside me.

I needed more time to get my head around it. Part of me wants this to be about growing our family. But when Q talks about the baby, and all their plans for being involved, it makes me realize that the kid will be part of our life. And as much as I want to nurture the kid, I don't want our lives to change the way a baby of our own would necessitate.

I want Q to always be comfortable as themself in the privacy of our home. If they had to go days or weeks without meaningful puppy time to put a kid's needs first, it wouldn't be ideal for either of us. They need their pupspace to thrive and I need to connect with them in that way.

When Q texts that they're leaving work and they'll see me soon, I'm waiting out front with a big bag of their favorite takeout foods. I love to pamper them, but the bag of their favorite treats is more of a personal penance. A salve to my guilt over not being as excited about this as Quent is. Or at least claims to be.

I'm not naïve enough to think they don't have mixed feelings, but they won't admit that without a fight because they seem convinced they should be happy. I text back, but they leave the pharmacy without responding.

At first Quent doesn't see me, so I call out the window to them. Their head whips around, like I startled the crap out of them. When they see it's me, they grin, wave, and make their way over to me with an uncharacteristic trudging droop to their shoulders. I thought I'd seen the last of that lackluster gait when we finally got their thyroid meds adjusted three years ago.

For Q to walk like that, instead of with their usual bounce, they truly are exhausted. That kicks my worry that we've made the wrong choice into high gear. Worry and resignation that we're in for a rough ride. I scrutinize their every move as I recalibrate my plans for the evening to take their physical state into account. We can still have fun. Take both our minds off what the next few months hold for us.

Quent opens the door, leans in, and breathes deep over the bag of greasy takeout. They inhale like they want to devour the meal with their nose first. Typical Quent, except instead of the pleased moan I expect and hope for, they gag violently and recoil out of the car. Not stopping there, they stagger toward a shrub at the edge of the parking lot to upchuck.

I'm out of the car and at their side in an instant, rubbing their back and murmuring softly to them. Q finishes puking, wipes the back of their hand over their mouth, and buries their face in my chest.

"Ugh. Mommy," they whine. I don't need to see their face to know they're pouting.

"Looks like this isn't the ticket to all you can eat cheese fries you were hoping for, puppy. I'm sorry." I rub their back. Q whimpers and nuzzles into me more insistently. Probably not ideal in the parking lot of their place of employment, no matter how progressive. "Come on, I'll dump the food and we can talk about it in the car."

"No, don't throw it out!" They lift their face, and sure enough, they are pouting at me.

"Just smelling it made you puke, Quentin. It isn't coming home with us." I caress their cheeks to soften the words. I'm not backing down on that though.

"Let me see if Al wants it. Even if my beloved cheese fries have betrayed me most cruelly, they still don't deserve to molder in a dumpster."

"Text her," I agree, then I take the bag out of the front seat and set it on the hood of the car so that Q can sit down. They do, with the door open so the aroma of fried food can dissipate. They still look green around the gills. I lean on their open door to watch them for signs of lingering illness.

"She'll be right out," Q assures me, bracing their elbows on their knees and propping their chin on their hands. "Am I going to feel like hot garbage for the next nine months? Like holy heck, it's barely showing up on a test and I'm already falling apart?"

"It's supposed to get better after the first trimester. And

upping your thyroid meds might help with symptoms."

"Yeah. I know. Doc said it might make those pesky issues come back. Annoying that my lazy thyroid doubles down on the pregnancy stuff." Q pouts at me.

"I know. Want to see if frozen yogurt is easier on your stomach?"

Q pouts at me. "The soft serve machines they use are supposed to be off limits. Because *Listeria*." They pull a yuck face.

"Well, then we'll just have to get a pint at the store and pick out some gummies to go on top."

"I guess." They sound glum. I hate that I can't fix this for them. Being helpless in the face of their misery is one of the worst things.

"You want to rest in the car while I shop?" I offer.

"Yes, please." Q forces a sweet smile for me.

"What do you want me to buy?" I ask. Quent perks up a bit as they list candies, which eases some of the guilt that I can't do more for them.

Alice steps out of the employee door at the back and strides over to us before we can finalize Q's list of required toppings. I step aside to let them talk.

"Hey, Q, you okay?" Alice asks as she takes the bag off the hood of the car and peeks inside. "Smells good."

"Normally I'd agree, but today, not so much." Q fakes gagging sounds. Alice looks concerned, so Q waves a hand. "I'm good. Take my delicious, cheesy betrayer and avenge me."

Alice quirks her head at Quent, then understanding dawns. "Ah, pregnancy aversions? My friend Emil swears by these ginger candies for nausea, just a sec and I'll grab you a pack. Laura works with one of his partners, so I've picked them up for him a few times."

"You don't have to."

"Nah, don't worry about it. I owe you one for the dinner, anyway." Alice hefts the bag. "Laura's gonna love coming home to a nice dinner neither of us has to cook. Thanks, you two. Wait right here and I'll get you the goods."

"Okay, thanks." Q hunches over their middle more.

Alice drops the bag of food off at her car and then returns to the pharmacy for the promised remedy.

"Think it will help?" I ask, since meds are their area of expertise and they've picked up a lot since working here.

"Can't hurt." Q shrugs.

"I mean, I'm pretty sure I can make ginger candies hurt plenty," I tease, leaning in close to kiss their crown.

"That isn't the threat you think it is. Although…let's skip the sugary candy and go right to the root itself."

"You asking for a figging, puppy?" I'm so tempted to tip their chin up for a proper kiss, but we're still in their work parking lot, so I refrain.

"Not today. Or probably any time soon. Ugh." Q curls their knees up to their chest and swivels in the chair to sit facing the windshield. "I think the smell is fading."

"Good. Watch your fingers," I warn, then I shut their door and go around to the driver's seat to wait for Alice. She hands Q the promised candies through the window and says goodnight and we head home, with a brief detour for frozen yogurt at the grocery store near our house.

That doesn't go down any easier than the fries. I end up making my pup toast, which they pick at, to go with their new favorite ginger candies. We make an early night of it, snuggled together in bed instead of the scene I'd had planned. The scene will keep, and both of us are happy to spend the night in each other's arms.

I just can't shake the sense that this is only the beginning of the ways the next few months will change things for us. I'd be lying if I said it doesn't worry me. My thoughts race along with my pulse as all the ways this could drive us apart run through my mind, unbidden.

I cling on tight to my pup. Quent might be the one with the insatiable sex drive, but I need them just as much as they need me, if in different ways. For once, I'm the one fingering their collar for reassurances that we're solid. Quent mumbles something, and their hand closes around mine, keeping me close.

CHAPTER 10
Kylee

Symptoms plague the early weeks of Q's pregnancy, leaving us both guessing if it's normal pregnancy stuff or a sign they need to increase their thyroid medications. They end up spending most of their early days off napping at my feet. Which is nice, if it weren't for the fact my poor pup is miserable.

At least the increase in their thyroid meds seems to help. Enough that they convince me not to cancel our play party the week after Adventures closes. I argue that, considering Q is expecting, it would be reasonable to reschedule. They disagree.

Q has been so down since the aversions started that I don't want to take another thing away from them. So I let the party proceed as planned, against my better judgment. Going against my protective instincts has me edgy the day of the party.

I normally handle everything, but I'm too tense to relax and play hostess, so we enlist more friends than usual to help run things the night of the party. I convince Quent to nap before our guests arrive, which they do without kicking up a fuss.

Connor comes early to help Q tidy the house. Hope volunteers to greet everyone at the door, and Clark offers to keep an extra eye on all the pups and their handlers so things don't get out of control. The party runs late into the night, but all the guests are people we know, so there's no trouble, despite my worries about overtaxing Quent.

The gathering is one of the largest we've hosted, so it's an enormous relief that Q has enough energy to enjoy it. I mingle less than my usual, worrying about them and trying not to fuss and ruin their night.

Organizing everything is stressful until our playroom is full of our community. Once the party is in full swing, I get to see my friends enjoying their evening in a space where they can all be free to be themselves. That feels pretty fantastic.

Several of the pups and Q's little friends look to me for care and guidance. I've mentored some of the other tops playing here tonight. I've played with most of these people in some capacity.

It's rewarding to give back, in some small way, to the community that welcomed me and gave me a home away from home. Especially since our usual play spaces aren't available to us this month between Adventures closing and our puppy mosh venue double booking our night.

Daisy, a new pup to the scene, runs around with Q until my pup is panting from exertion and I order them to my side to rest and hydrate. I nudge Cara, a handler who lost her pup to an accident last year and seems to be ready to meet someone new, toward Daisy.

The pup is new to puppy play, but not the broader leather scene. The two of them seem to hit it off. Daisy and Cara aren't the only new couple I see spending an awful lot of time together over the course of the night. Rory stays glued to Tate's side, doting on the little. And I spy Con and Jax coming out of the washroom together later in the evening.

Quent wears themself out pretty thoroughly by the end of the night. I'm still glad we went through with the party. Glad I made time to connect with friends and be social. Sometimes that gets lost in the shuffle between so much of our play centering around Quent's needs and my working from home, so I don't get out much. The party provides a refreshing chance to unwind that I need more than I knew.

Quent has to call in sick to work the next morning, but our party is the happiest I've seen them since sharing the positive test result with Jared and Logan. It's also the first time they show an interest in sex since the test.

They're half-asleep when I bring them up to bed. But they rouse enough to offer me oral, which they perform with lazy, languid strokes of their tongue. Q's eyelids are so droopy they almost have me convinced they'll fall asleep before I finish if I take too long.

They don't fall asleep, but their usual enthusiasm is lacking. When they yawn mid-oral, I give up on orgasms in favor of exchanging sleepy kisses with them.

Quent pushes my hands away when I touch anywhere near their chest, with a whined complaint that they're too tender. I don't push, of course I don't, but I miss the warmth of their breath on my skin when they turn their back to me to sleep. It's like a confirmation of my worst fears.

***

In the month since the night of our play party, Quent's stamina and morning sickness have both improved steadily. Everything except their food aversions, those appear to be here to stay. And them not wanting me to touch their chest only gets worse with time. I get why, but it still slams into me like a loss when their hugs become more reserved.

Their constant desire for physical affection is a staple in my life, and I miss it when they pull back. I miss knowing that every part of them is mine and very little is truly off limits between us. For now, they've got boundaries they haven't had with me in the past. It stings.

I knew to expect the pregnancy to come with a heaping

helping of dysphoria. It's still hard that they don't want me to help them in the ways they normally crave from me. I don't mean to pull back from them in response. It's just that it hurts when they turn away from me. Like having a piece of my heart torn out.

At least their fatigue improving means we can keep busy and distracted from all the physical changes that are coming our way. I plan several more parties. It's one way to overcome my apprehensions about the next several months of dealing with this pregnancy and preserve a sense of normalcy. Holding events is my best effort at filling in the gaps in our social life that Adventures' closure created.

I've also got several munches we're responsible for organizing on our schedule. Nothing so large as the party after Adventure's closed, but still plenty to do. Martin, the club's owner and a close friend, is on the invite list for our next party. So it's fortuitous that he calls me about a month after the club closes.

We haven't chatted recently, beyond a terse message exchange through my business account about updating the club's website with the closure news. I'm sure he could handle that on his end if he was so inclined and not overwhelmed, but I didn't mind a quick project to help him out. The tone of our emails made it clear he was scrambling to handle all the issues the sudden closure caused. I don't take his lack of social calls in the immediate aftermath personally, but it's still nice to hear from him when he does eventually pick up the phone.

"How are you coping?" I ask once he's given me the rundown on everything that's gone wrong since the pipe burst and ruined his office last month.

Martin sighs heavily. "You know, you might be the first person who asked me that?"

He doesn't pause long enough for me to reply, but I'd have waited him out for an actual answer even if he had. That's just what I do; taking care of everyone around me comes naturally to me. It's a trait that brings up fond memories of my mother.

"I'm still in crisis mode. Adventures is my baby. It's one of the last pieces of Charlie that I have left. I mean, I'll always have Tabby, but she's graduating. It's like I'm losing both of my babies at the same time. So I haven't really given myself time to process. I'm just doing what I can to make sure we reopen. Bigger and better than ever, you know?"

"Makes sense. I'm here for you, if you need me. All of us are. If you need a shoulder to cry on, a friend to drown your sorrows with you, or a Domme to help you find release, I'm happy to oblige. And if you'd rather torture out your feelings, I've got an eager puppy to take whatever you want to dish out to them." I wince internally after making that offer.

It's not that Q wouldn't be more than happy for me to arrange a playdate with Martin, though they aren't always a fan of his rougher play preferences. Or that they would begrudge sharing me with him for a few hours.

No, I regret it because I'm not used to factoring their pregnancy into our scenes with other people. I'll need to look into what is and isn't acceptable for them, beyond our usual routine. And we need to discuss how we want to deal with disclosing the pregnancy to our friends and play partners. This is going to take even more mental adjustment on my part.

Martin chuckles at the other end of the line. "You've got my number when it comes to preferred coping mechanisms. There *is* someone I've got my eye on for blowing off some steam. We'll see if he's as interested as I suspect. He perks up whenever he overhears me mention Adventures. But I'll keep your offer in mind. You and Quent are always fun to play with. I mostly called to vent about the difficulty of finding a kink friendly contractor. Figured you might commiserate after your playroom remodel a while back."

"Sure, we used Reynolds' Construction. Harry, the owner, customized our playroom between commercial projects and we loved his work. Very kink positive. He and Q hit it off and they've kept in touch. He runs their D&D game. Want me to pass along his information? I don't think he's in the lifestyle, but Q's toys didn't phase him in the least."

"He's the DM they mentioned inviting into the club during off hours for their game sessions? Oh, just a moment," Martin says, then his voice becomes muffled, like he moved his phone away from his face instead of muting the call. He's not the most tech savvy of my clients and friends, so that's entirely in character. "I'd love a refill, thanks." Martin mentioned working from a cafe this week. That could explain where he had the time to meet a new potential boy in the whirlwind of the club's closing. There's some rustling, and then Martin returns to the call. "Sorry about that. I'll give your guy a call. Thanks for the suggestion. You're a lifesaver, Ky."

"Nah, that was my summer job ages ago. Unless you're calling me tart and fruity?" I tease.

"More like sweet as sugar, dearheart. How are you and Q?" It's the first time in a while someone has asked me that, and I'm sorely tempted by the offer.

I consider unburdening myself to Martin. He's always been a friend and confidant, but we haven't discussed telling him about the pregnancy yet. I take a middle ground. "We're alright. Q is adjusting to some dose changes with their meds, so we're in a bit of a rough patch, but we'll get through it. I'm struggling with them needing me when there's nothing I can do to make it better. And we normally talk about these things, but talking won't make them feel better faster; only time will do that."

"I'm sorry to hear it. I've been there with Charlie before she passed. Let me know if there's anything I can do to help? You deserve support, too, yeah? Don't you wallow in guilt over that."

The genuine concern in Martin's voice warms something in me I've been trying to ignore. And hearing that he's been there too assuages some of my guilt over having selfish desires that are at odds with what Q needs from me. I can't always be just their Mommy to the exclusion of my own needs for connection and love.

"Thanks, I will." I clutch the phone harder, resolving to follow through on that promise when he's less busy with the remodel. "And I'll find Harry's business card and message you the details."

"Thanks, and thanks for whipping up the changes to the website. Love the graphic you used. It's perfect."

"Not a problem. I'll pass along your thanks to Jax for the spiffy pics."

"Perfect. I'll be in touch once I get everything coordinated," Martin promises. We wrap up the conversation. I make a note to send along Harry's information once I finish what I was working on when Martin called.

I add another note to double check the kinds of play that will be off limits while Q is pregnant. Of course, I did some preliminary research, but it never hurts to stay on top of things. Especially since my stubborn pup is getting over their earlier fatigue and the worst of the nausea now that they've got their thyroid dose adjusted. They're eager for a scene. And I hope that planning something we both enjoy will help us reconnect.

I had my doubts about Q's mental health through this process, but so far, they are handling everything as well as can be expected. The dysphoria and doubled up sports bras I have to pry them out of at bedtime notwithstanding.

Our doctor vetoed binders while gestating and the pregnancy hormones are taking their toll on Q's chest. It's not a huge change, but enough to bother them. Most of their front is off limits during sex and snuggles these days. Still, I expected that to be an issue and the light compression seems to make it tolerable for them.

Even without the full picture, Martin is right that I've been guilty about my reactions lately and neglecting my needs to compensate for that guilt. It's hard for me to accept I can't do much about their dysphoria, other than giving Quent ways to take their mind off of it. And if a scene seems like the best way for us to connect as well as a needed distraction for them, well, that can only be a good thing.

I just need to adjust my plans to suit their changing body. Which means scouring message boards and lurking around kinky pregnancy forums to get the first hand scoop on any alterations we need to make to accommodate our growing nibling. It can't hurt to be prepared and part of that means knowing what scenes are safe and what's off limits until the baby arrives.

I give up on finishing the piece of code I was working on, save the project, and fall down a research rabbit hole for the rest of the day. My preliminary searches left me satisfied we won't have to give up most of our favorite types of play. Further poking around now that we're in the thick of it gives me tips and tricks to adapt what we do for Q as things progress. The suggestions for taking extra care of my pregnant pup actually appeal to me more than I would've thought.

I never considered caring for a pregnant Quentin before they brought up surrogacy. Probably because neither of us actually wants kids. The past while caring for them as they've dealt with morning sickness, and rubbing their sore feet at the end of a long day at work, holds a certain appeal.

This whole thing might be a great way to reinvigorate our relationship. Break out of our usual routines and show my affection in new and meaningful ways. I like that prospect. Better than my helplessness to fix this situation as they put physical distance between us.

The constant tension and sense of loss I've felt eases as I come up with a list of new ways that we can still be close. I've been viewing this from the perspective of what we can't do right now, but that isn't helpful. We need to talk. And for Q to open up, they need the safety net of my love.

Hopefully, if we can reclaim our physical intimacy in new ways, we'll both find it easier to open up and share how the pregnancy is affecting us. I miss being able to tell what they're thinking and where their head is at more than almost anything since we started down this road.

I text Martin a picture of Harry's card, do some online shopping for soothing scents of massage oil and bubble bath to offer my pup a bit of pampering. Q is going to love every second of what I've got planned for them. It will be worth working late tonight catching up on the project sitting ignored on my desktop to give my pup whatever comfort I can while they're feeling crummy. I need to find a way back to our usual closeness, and perhaps a new bubble bath or massage oil will do the trick.

When Q gets home, they greet me with their usual enthusiasm, barreling into my arms with a chirpy greeting.

"Hi, Mommy." They beam up at me, and I wrap them in a tight embrace.

There's nothing better than an armful of smiling Q. My bouncy ball of excited puppy is enough to tear me away from the work I should be finishing for a break. We both ignore their sudden wince when I brush against their chest by accident.

"Hello to you too, pup. Want spaghetti with pesto for dinner?" I suggest.

It's quick and hasn't triggered their all too frequent nausea so far. "I still have some work to finish up after we eat."

"I can do pasta." Quent pouts about my having to work, but they don't comment on it.

I put on the water to boil while Q gets out the dry noodles and a jar of pre-made sauce. We have dinner together, exchanging stories about our days. I mention my talk with Martin. Quent tells me the latest work gossip, which mostly seems to be about their coworker, Alice, adopting a kitten with her girlfriend. Said kitten has a penchant for stealing all unattended beverages.

"I'm trying to convince Al to name the kitten Rapscallion." They end the story as they finish the last bite of their meal. They suck on their fork and look mournfully at the empty plate. "Do you really have to work more?"

"I really do. Sorry, puppy. Do you want to sit with me?"

"Yes, please."

"Can you be a good pup while you wait for Mommy to finish her work?" I arch a brow in challenge, knowing their competitive drive more than anything will guarantee their good behavior.

Q nods, wriggling in their seat like they want to wag their tail at me.

"Let's go then." I gather up our dirty dishes and set them in the sink to deal with later. Q follows me to my office on all fours. I drag in their favorite napping spot, an oversized dog bed they picked in the days before they got their thyroid issues diagnosed.

Before their meds, my poor pup needed daily naps to function at all. Now they enjoy the occasional nap, but it's not the necessary part of our day that it once was. I don't miss them being miserable and not knowing why they felt crappy all the time, but I missed those naps when they stopped happening.

I love having my pup asleep at my feet while I work. That's one thing I've enjoyed about the past few weeks with Q. Letting them watch their favorite show on their phone while they lean against me is the next best thing to a sleepy puppy curled up at my feet. It hasn't been all bad. I need to remember that more.

I watch Q settle into their dog bed out of the corner of my eye as I open up the neglected project from earlier. Q gets comfy, resting their chin on the toe of my boot. They nudge me until I start the show on their phone and prop it up where they can see it. I wear my headphones to tune out the sounds of dogs going on adventures with their human companions.

I absently reach down to pet Q's head every so often. If I wasn't wearing my favorite comfy indoor boots, I might have run my foot along their back in a caress. But the soles are rough, and I don't want to hurt Quent with them.

It's not the worst way to work late. They paw at my ankle when the show stops with a message asking if they're still watching. I press the button to keep streaming and Q settles in, licking at my hand in appreciation. They shift to lapping at my ankle when I take my hand back to keep working.

Hours pass with my pup patiently waiting for me to finish. I get to the point I'd planned to be at today for this project, save it, and shut down the computer. Q makes a happy little bark and rolls onto their belly, then pushes up to position themself between my thighs, they nose at me eagerly.

"Not right now, pup." I lean down to kiss their mouth.

Q sighs into the kiss. It's not that I don't want them. I do. I'm just not in the mood for sex and I need a minute to switch off from work.

And if I'm honest, I'm tired. I love being their Mommy, but the past month has been hard. They've needed me more than usual and they've shut me out because of their chest growing. I've tried to be there for them and I understand they're going through something huge. But sometimes I need a chance to just be Kylee and not always have everything resting on my shoulders.

Surrogacy is hard in ways I didn't even anticipate, and I resent that it's pushed us apart and put a strain on our relationship. Some days it seems like little has changed. Other days it's like pregnancy has stolen my playful pup from me and left me with an irritable partner who doesn't want to be touched.

Tonight is one of the former days. Where they're more like their usual happy self. They whine plaintively when I pull back and pet their head to placate them. Guilt almost makes me buckle and offer them whatever they want, but I just don't have it in me tonight. I know what they want, but I need a minute.

"Get your chewie if you need something in your mouth. I'm ready for bed."

Q pads off to fetch their favorite toy while I unlace the leather boots I wear to work from home. It's one of those weird rituals that helps me differentiate between being home to relax and being on work time.

Finding shoes that make me feel powerful and femme at the same time is always a rush. No less so because I have to order from specialized stores to get my size. So now that I work from home, having dedicated work shoes is an empowering way to get in the right headspace.

And bonus points, because the boots in question were made to be worshiped by my mouthy pup. It's much easier to keep them clean enough for said pup to lick when I don't wear them out of the house. That can wait for another night, since they need to be up for work in the morning and it's getting late.

Q returns and noses at the boots as though they also regret the lack of time to give them attention. They lean in to swipe their tongue over my stocking-covered toes and I yelp at the ticklish heat of their mouth before pushing them away. It's so them that

I can't help but smile. They always know how to wear me down with their playfulness. Their sweet energy has brought me out of many a funk.

"None of that, pup. It's bedtime," I scold.

Q leans their head against my thigh for pats. I crouch to lavish them in kisses and cuddles, getting my face thoroughly covered in eager puppy licks. It's just what I need to remind myself why I love being with them. This is how they show me they appreciate all the little things I do for them as their Mommy. And really, I think that's what I've been most upset about.

Coming from Quent, getting pushed away is tantamount to rejection. It's been making me feel unappreciated these past few months. What they're doing now—lapping at my face like I'm their favorite person in the world and they can't contain their joy at having my undivided attention—goes a long way to showing their love.

Quent as a pup is unbridled joy and enthusiasm for life. They are uncomplicated affection. There's not an ounce of artifice in them; they just adore me so much they can't hold it all in.

And I can't be mad at them. Or resentful of their needs. They aren't asking for anything I didn't promise. I'm just having a hard time adjusting to change.

"Bedtime," I insist again, because rules are still rules. "If you want your treat at the munch next week, you need to be a good pup. That means going to bed on time, Q. I'll be up once I handle the dishes and fix your lunch for tomorrow." The reminder that their favorite cheesy fries are on the line usually does the trick, but I forgot how sick fried food has made them since they got knocked up.

Q pouts at me, whining miserably.

"Sorry. I know. But you've been less sick, so perhaps if we try again at the munch, you'll be able to stomach some fries? And if not, there's always dessert." Sweets don't seem to make them sick. Mollified, Quent yips agreeably, then licks my hand. "You won't get any type of treat if you don't get to bed, now, puppy." I put on my sternest tone. Quent huffs a disgruntled bark, then galumphs up the stairs on all fours, racing me to our bed.

The evidence that their boundless energy has returned makes me smile as I go to handle my last few responsibilities for the day. It's a glimpse of our normal. A glimmer of hope that we can get through this stronger than ever. I'm more hopeful now that I have a plan in place to be intentional about staying connected.

That smile stays with me as I pack their lunch for tomorrow. This is one way I get to take care of Quent. They typically get up first, so they make the morning coffee for us both, but I prep the filter and make sure we have a clean travel mug for their commute.

I quickly wash our dinner dishes and assemble some of Q's favorite foods to put in their lunchbox. This way, it will be ready for them to grab from the fridge in the morning. Tonight I pay attention to the tiny details that show I love them. Cutting their sandwich with a dog-shaped bread cutter I know will make them smile and adding in some of their favorite bone-shaped cookies we made together over the weekend. I even slip a short love note into the bag, like I used to do before I let the little gestures get lost in the bustle of our day-to-day routines.

By the time I get upstairs and brush my teeth, Q is curled up on my pillow, fast asleep. They mumble a groggy protest when the bed shifts as I join them under the covers, but they only rouse enough to snuggle into me.

Even in their sleep, they find their rightful place plastered against my side with ease. They nuzzle their face into the crook of my neck, their forgotten chewie wedged between us. I'm thankful to have their familiar warmth next to me.

I truly hope this is a sign that things are going to be okay between us. And I'm going to do everything in my power to make sure that it is. We can build on these good days and open up about how we're both struggling.

There is a lot we still need to discuss. I need them to open up about how the pregnancy is affecting them, because I can tell that it is, but I'll take a reprieve. One good night can't fix what's been brewing between us, but it's a first step that gives me hope for our future.

CHAPTER 11

Quent

Somehow, the first trimester is over and we're already going in for an NT scan. I teased Jar and Logan about wanting the test as an excuse to get early baby pics. I think the real reason they insisted is because they don't want to get too attached if the baby has something wrong that isn't compatible with life. That happened to them with an adoption that fell through, so I get their worry.

It's not like they can share in all my little daily reminders of their kid growing inside me to reassure them all is well. Mommy and I had to go shopping for stretchy pants last weekend because my work slacks don't quite button comfortably anymore. I don't mind that as much as the curves it's added to my figure.

My chest is a nightmare every time I catch sight of it. I just don't look like me anymore. It makes my skin crawl every time I notice it. Which hasn't helped with my moodiness at all. Neither did the fact that all the pregnancy wear is super gendered and mom-centric, which doesn't work for me on multiple levels.

All that to say, I'm pretty sure the kid is growing just fine. But it will sure be nice to see an almost fully formed healthy little human, just to be sure I'm not subjecting myself to all of this over more heartache. I'm hoping seeing a healthy baby in there will ease some of my anxiety that something might go wrong.

I chose an ultrasound clinic that my coworkers swear is queer friendly. Since Al knows not one, but two other trans people who are both due this summer, I've been getting all kinds of second-hand pregnancy recs from her.

Not going to lie, it's helped to know I'm not the only one who willingly did this to myself. So far, other than the food aversions, the hardest part has been needing a bra. Binding while my chest was already aching proved to be a no-go. At least I'm still an A-cup—for now. The fact the changes are still minimal hasn't stopped me from squirming in the bad way when Mommy touches me there.

I know the physical distance I've needed to cope with that hurts her. She tries not to show it, but I can see and I hate making her sad. I hate the reflexive need to deny her access to any part of me. Of course, we've always had boundaries, but this one strikes me as wrong. Because I don't want it to be a boundary. I want to offer all of myself to her like usual, so it sucks that I can't handle it right now.

I only hope it will be a short-term change. Something I can give her again once the baby is here. The alternative tears me up inside every time I recoil at her touch. It's hurting us both and I haven't been able to figure out a way to talk about that hurt, since I can't change it.

Part of me wants to push through the churning in my gut when I expose the changes to her to give her the closeness we usually share. I need to see that we can go back to normal, even if it's uncomfortable at first.

The staff at the clinic lives up to Alice's rave reviews. They greet us with non-gendered language and introduce themselves using their pronouns, so it's easier to share mine. And once we explain our situation, the tech lets both the dads-to-be in to watch the proceedings. It ranks among my less traumatic medical visits.

Ky offered to come along for moral support, but that

would have made for a cramped exam room. Besides, between regular lab draws to assess my meds, prenatal visits, and my symptoms making her all protective of me, she could use some uninterrupted work time.

Instead, Jar holds my hand while the sonographer does her thing. I watch Jared's face as the static on the screen displays my insides. Weird. Logan rests his head on Jar's shoulder and squeezes my brother tight as the monotone blurs resolve into the outline of a tiny face in profile. The peek inside their intimacy makes me miss Kylee with a visceral longing.

The picture makes this all the more real. That's my nibling lounging on their back. Kid looks cool as a cucumber floating in their own personal pool. It's weird how much I already adore that big forehead and cute little nose. I can't wait to kiss the stuffing out of this kid. The dainty chin tipped toward their tubby belly reminds me of Jar.

The sonographer takes the measurements she needs in short order. I still wish I'd taken Mommy up on her offer to be here.

"Want to hear the baby's heartbeat?" She offers. The guys jump at the chance and soon the rapidfire lub-dubs filter through the speakers. And I feel like my heart is racing to catch up with that beat at the reality of what I'm doing.

"Whoa." Logan looks awestruck.

His smile makes his entire face glow, as besotted as it was the day he and Jared got hitched. Jared squeezes Logan's hand and glances between me and his husband. His smile is just as mushy as Logan's. It makes me miss Mommy even more. I wish she was here. Even though I told her it was okay if she skipped today's appointment.

I'm not okay without her. I need her, and I need to find a way to tell her that. To show her I need her with me, even when I push her away.

"That's our kid." Jared turns his focus back to the screen, hungry for every moment he gets to look.

"I've got what I need. If you want to clean up, I'll print out some pictures for you to take home and your doctor will call about the full results."

"Thanks." I take the tissues she hands me and scrub at my belly. Now that I've seen the kid, it's weird to have visual confirmation that there's really a tiny human in there. I'd rather not think about it. I lie back on the table, gathering myself.

"You okay, sib?" Jared rubs my arm.

"Yeah. Just. It's so weird to think about having a whole human in me. Like, extreme fisting," I joke to hide my nerves.

"Gross." Jared slugs my shoulder playfully. "You did not just turn our kid into a kink. You're such a weirdo."

I sputter a bit at that, because I definitely turned the actual conception into a kink. And I'm not even a little sorry about it because that was one of the hottest scenes ever. Before I can respond, the sonographer knocks and comes back in with the pictures. She hands them to Logan with another congratulations, and leaves.

Logan takes one look at the pictures and guffaws.

"What?" Jared turns and reaches for the strip of photos.

"Nothing, just speaking of fisting..." Logan points to the third image where the baby is waving a computer labeled fist at us. I can't help laughing too.

"Pregnancy is trippy." I pull up the stretchy waistband on my preggo pants and fix my shirt over them before hopping awkwardly down from the exam table. The two layers of sports bras ride up uncomfortably and I hate them almost as much as the chest growth the baby has inspired. But then I look at the wide smiles on Jared and Logan's faces as they coo over their baby and I can't be mad about it. "Let me see my precious nibling. I need pics to show Aunty Ky."

I snatch the photos from my brother and lay them out on the exam table where I was sitting. He doesn't protest as I snap a picture on my phone to send to Ky and Connor. Logan takes a snap to send to his extended family too. Then Jared takes the pictures back. Sharing this moment with Mommy helps ease the ache in my heart, even if she's too busy to reply right away.

"Thanks," Jared says as he carefully takes the printout from me. I get the impression he means for more than the pictures.

I nudge our shoulders together. "You're welcome. Now, I believe you mentioned something about lunch?"

"Yep, ramen it is, if you can stand the wait," Jared teases me.

"For the best soup in the city? Yeah, I'll deal. At least your kid still lets me enjoy soup." I stick my tongue out at him.

Jared wraps an arm around my shoulder as we walk out of the exam room. He kisses my temple before we separate at the door. Logan takes his husband's hand for the short walk from the ultrasound clinic to the popular ramen place. The two of them keep me in their loop, even though part of me felt like the outsider while I was lying on the exam table getting prodded.

It would be easy for the two of them to go be a family with their kid when this is over. And they will. But just like when I moved out of Jared's place, and later moved in with Mommy, that doesn't make me any less a part of Jared's life and family. It just looks different. And adding this kid to the equation will shift things again. That makes my chest tight. I hope it's a good shift. So far, it's drawing us closer. We always keep in touch, but I've been texting with them both daily lately instead of weekly.

As we walk, we chat about the latest board game they want to play with Mommy and me at our next family game night.

Jared ribs his husband because Logan picked up a second copy of Zombies!!! on clearance. He's a sucker for all things zombies and the illustration on the PG edition box appealed to him.

I tease Logan about that. He gives as good as he gets, pointing out that the family friendly version of the game is better for the future kid. That logic gets Jared and me both to concede his point, even though the baby is years away from being ready for board games.

I can picture playing games with them, Mommy, and my nibling. Once they're old enough for that. We need to look into gateway games to get the kid hooked. I'm so here for that future. I rub a hand over the barely there bump. This kid feels so much more real than they have up to this point. Jared notices the move and bumps elbows with me, just to touch and connect.

"Know what soup you want?" he asks, because he knows me and he knows I don't want him to make a bigger deal of the whole thing. The three of us debate the merits of the various menu options until it's our turn to be seated for the best soup in town.

It's a good day. A perfect reminder of why I'm putting myself through this whole pregnancy ordeal. I just wish Kylee had been a part of it too. I wish I knew how to fix the distance growing between us. She means the world to me, and I know it's my fault. I want to fix it, if only I knew how. As I'm heading home, I see a storefront display that might help. If I can stand the discomfort. A way to show her I'm trying. A gesture to prove I still belong to her, no matter what.

CHAPTER 12

Kylee

When Quent gets home after the NT scan and lunch, they come into my office without knocking. I don't expect them to if I'm not with a client. They plop down into their napping spot with barely a word of greeting.

I have to tear my eyes away from their chest. I could swear it looks more pronounced than when they left this morning. They look hot. Which is not a sentiment my pup would appreciate. I shake my head at the distraction and put those thoughts, and the desire they stir, out of my mind.

Quent props their chin on my toe. I minimize the indie movie nerd forum I was catching up on between projects. They always claim they aren't into my favorite low-budget productions, but that hasn't ever stopped them from curling up with me in our den when I want to watch one.

Even though Quent listens when I talk about movies, I prefer to discuss them with people who actually appreciate film the same way that I do. So I'm active in the forums. It's one of the few places where I haven't stepped into some ongoing role with added responsibility and there's something freeing about that too. Just getting to enjoy a casual interest.

Taking a few minutes to do something just for me helped me grapple with the feelings the grainy images of our nibling triggered when Quent sent me the ultrasound pictures. That tide of emotions made me glad I didn't go in person. It was a lot to grapple with and I'm glad they didn't see my grief over everything the picture symbolizes.

The baby in those images has a piece of Quent in them, and it hit me hard to realize that we're giving that to someone else. Yes, it's someone Quent loves. And I love Jared and Logan too. I want them to have the family they've dreamed of, but it's a lot to wrap my head around.

I expected Quent's pregnancy to be hard. But I was unprepared for the constant tangible reminder that there are parts of what is generally considered womanhood I'll never experience. It's been getting to me more than I thought it would.

That's far from a uniquely trans experience. If reading up on fertility forums to prepare for this taught me nothing else, it's that treating motherhood as some pinnacle of femininity does all women a disservice. I'm far from the first woman to ache over the lack of a functioning uterus. I won't be the last to yearn for an experience that isn't in the cards for me.

In my head, I know it shouldn't define me. Just like being pregnant doesn't define who Quent is. That's what I'd tell every single one of the other women posting on those forums, mourning over something that seems to come so easily to so many other people. No matter how much I know those things in my head, it still hurts to see Quent struggle with changes I would treasure.

It's more than my newly awakened dysphoria over something I thought I'd come to peace with years ago that's bothering me. It's that a part of me—however small—wonders what it would be like to raise a child with Quent. Realistically, I know it isn't part of our plans for the future. But between my unexpected attachment to the baby-to-be and their excitement about spoiling our nibling, I've been second-guessing that decision.

When we were discussing the surrogacy arrangement, both

men assured us that Q and I would always have a place in the baby's life. I have to remember that. And I have to remember that Quent doesn't want to be a parent. That was never a secret. They love kids, but they don't want to be responsible for them full time. And truthfully, neither do I.

I've got so many other responsibilities, that isn't something I want to take on. But it's still hitting me hard. Maybe I'm projecting, but Q seems sad today too.

"Is everything alright?" I ask when Quent curls up and rests their chin more firmly on my boot, clearly wanting to be close without disturbing my work. I scruff their ears.

"Yeah. The baby seemed healthy. I sent you the pics," Q deflects.

"I saw. You seem down."

"It's nothing big." They yawn theatrically and snuggle closer to me, curling up tighter. "Napping now. You're busy. I want you to finish your work and we'll talk later."

"If you're sure, but we *are* talking tonight." I give them one more pat and pull up my work project.

"Mhm, night, Mommy."

"Sleep well, pup." I turn my attention back to my computer while they take their nap at my feet. Q sleeps fitfully. Whatever is bothering them seems to have followed them into their dreams and they move around more than usual in their sleep, even whimpering a few times. I long to wake them and pull them into my arms. What stops me is that I don't think I could take the emotional blow if they reject my efforts at comforting them. That's something they've been doing more and more lately.

It's hard to focus on my work instead of waking them to deal with their worries, but they aren't wrong that I have deadlines. If they need a nap, or time to process before we discuss the problem, then I'll give them their space.

Quent sleeps through the end of my workday. I put in an order for the veggie burritos they've been craving pretty much daily for the past few weeks rather than disturbing them to get dinner cooking. Then I scroll my film forums until the doorbell heralds our food arriving. The sound wakes them with a startled little bark that makes me laugh.

"Good dreams?" I ask, carefully pushing my chair back to get up without stepping on them.

Q stretches, then sits up with a grimace and wipes drool from their chin. They yawn again. "Who's here?"

"Dinner."

"Mm. Pizza?" They guess with a hopeful smile.

"Close. I got burritos." I rise to get the door.

"Yummy. You think of everything." Quent trails after me, still looking adorably sleepy and rumpled.

They really do glow. Their loose shirt obscures their new curves as they walk, and I'm struck by a pang at the unfairness of it. That both of us struggle with parts of our bodies the other aches to have. Most of the time, it's not something that bothers me these days. I've changed what I can and made peace with what I can't. But seeing Quent struggle is hard, and having them push me away because of those struggles is harder.

"Yep. Want to eat in the den and talk about what's bothering you?" I should also tell them what's bothering me. I know they realize I've been having a hard time with this too.

"Sure. I'll get utensils and stuff." They stop in the kitchen to grab what we need and I collect our food and tip our delivery driver. When I bring our burritos into the den, Quent is already on the couch with our TV trays set up.

I distribute the food and sit next to them in the place they prepared for me. Quent digs into the food with a happy moan. I smile at how much they enjoy their food, glad that their upset hasn't dampened their usual enthusiasm, at least.

"So?" I ask once they've taken several large bites.

Quent shrugs and sets their half-eaten burrito gingerly on their plate. "So. I guess seeing the ultrasound made it seem more real? That and shopping for clothes the other day and seeing how big my chest is getting with the bright lights and mirrors in the changing room. And I hate having to wear a bra, even if it's just to compress things and make me flat." They fuss with their bra. The straps look narrower than what they've been wearing.

"I'm sorry, pup." I bite back empty reassurances about their chest, knowing full well that their dysphoria can't be reasoned or complimented away. "We can shop online for anything else you need."

"Yeah. I'd prefer that." They pluck at their loose shirt where it clings to their curves and make a yuck face. "Guess I'll need to switch to the even baggier stuff. Mind if I go change real quick?"

"Not at all. Are you going to come back down to finish dinner or want me to pack this up for your lunch tomorrow?"

Quent considers, then gives me an apologetic shrug. "Put it in my lunch. I ate late with the guys, so I'm not super hungry. Might try to take a bath and relax."

"Sure. Let me take care of things down here, and then I'll come up and help you relax." I imbue the last word with a hint of suggestion.

"Mm. That sounds nice," They agree, then they lean into my space for a quick kiss.

I want to pull them into my lap and make all their worries disappear, but I settle for kissing them soundly and swatting their ass playfully when they pull free. That makes them grin at me as they make a show of walking away.

"Don't take too long," they throw back over their shoulder.

As if I didn't already have all the incentive I need to follow them upstairs. I finish eating, take care of Quent's leftovers, and get the kitchen ready for our morning routine in record time.

When I let myself into our steamy en suite, Q is neck deep in bubbles and the cloying scent of floral body wash fills the air. I wrinkle my nose and Q laughs.

"Yeah." They copy my expression. "I know, but this is all we have left. Guess I used up the last of the lavender one you ordered. Dug this one up from the back of the cabinet. I guess there's a reason we never used it."

They laugh when I unceremoniously drop the rest of the bottle into the bin. I glimpse something lacy crumpled under the bottle. Odd. "I'll pick up more of the ones you like tomorrow."

"I can grab some at work." They wave off my offer, and the realization I've gotten numb to these brush offs lately sends me reeling. "You've seriously been pampering the crap out of me, Ky. I can get my own bubble bath."

"You *can*. But I enjoy taking care of you, Quentin."

Quent shudders at the nickname. "Mommy?"

"Yes?"

"I like when you call me that." They prod at some bubbles, unable to meet my gaze.

"I know." I smile at them.

It's not just the name, it's that our home is their safe space where they can just be my Q. I regret not going with them to the appointment today. I should have been there to be sure no one misgendered my pup or made them uncomfortable. Or whatever else happened to dampen their usual cheer. Even if it hurt me to think about seeing a baby on the screen and knowing it wasn't ours.

I take a seat on the closed toilet lid to be closer to them. "Want me to scrub your back?"

"Sure. Wash my hair too?" They turn their back to me.

"You're sure everything went well today?" I find a clean cup to scoop water over their head so I can lather up their hair.

Quent waits until I finish wetting their hair to reply, "yeah. The clinic people were as awesome as Alice said they'd be. My chest is just bothering me. A lot. It's jiggly." They pout with their entire body as they say that last word. I have to bite back my amusement at their theatrics. They're adorable, but I don't want them to think I'm making light of their concerns.

"I'm sorry it's bothering you so much." I run their washcloth over their shoulders, taking care to be gentle with the faint red marks on their shoulders. Irritated lines where they wore their bra straps too tight to compress the area in question.

Quent sighs, flinching from the touch. "Me too. I'm worried that if it's already this crappy, that by the end it will be too awful to bear."

"Does this hurt?"

"Yeah. While I was out today, I thought it could be fun to wear something pretty for you; ya know, if I have to deal with these." They gesture sharply toward their chest with a splash of bubbles. "Didn't go as planned, just made me hyper-aware of them. I got rid of it." They cut their eyes toward the lacy something hanging out of the trash. Ah, that explains it. "The sports bras are better. Almost comfy even."

"I appreciate the thought, puppy. You didn't have to do that for me." I finish washing their back, touched by the effort, and rinse their hair. "Want me to wash the rest of you?"

"Uh, huh. I wanted to do it. You're always doing nice things for me. I just couldn't." Quent splashes around to face me and gestures for me to go ahead with the scrubbing. I do as they ask, but when I run the washcloth over their chest, they crumple forward and shake their head. They grip my wrist tight to keep me from touching them. "Nope. Sorry. I can't." Their voice is panicky and they shake their head.

I withdraw my hand and try not to show that my wrist stings when they clearly didn't mean to hurt me. "Don't be sorry. It's fine. I get it, Q."

"I want you to touch me, Mommy. More than I can say. I just..." They splash helplessly in frustration.

"Can't handle being touched there right now," I finish for them.

"Yeah. That. It's like they're super sensitive and I can sense people looking at them, let alone touching." They slouch down under the water until the bubbles are up to their nose.

"Is it only your chest that's bothering you?" I keep my tone soft.

"Physically? Yeah, it's mostly just there for now. Worried about telling people, but the baggier stuff we got at the store should let me put that off a while longer. Not a huge fan of how the hormones are changing my junk and the way I get turned on, but I can still get off, so that's not too bad."

"Do you want to talk about it? Or is there anything else specific I should know?" Telling people is an issue we will have to tackle eventually. For now, I don't want to push too hard all at once. I'm just thrilled that they're finally opening up to me. This could be the breakthrough we've both needed.

"It's just different. I'm not sure how to describe it. Well, I mean, I guess moist?" They pull a face. "Makes it feel less like me. It even smells wrong."

"That's not fun. I'm sorry this is hard for you."

"At least I'm over a third of the way through." They try to find a bright side. Ever the optimist, my puppy. They bring so much brightness into my life every day. "Do you have anything you need to talk about? I know this has changed things for both of us." Quent asks me.

And even more than opening up to me, that's what I've been waiting for. A tension I've been carrying around since we started this journey loosens. They're actually ready to talk this out with me, all of it. As long as we keep our communications open, I truly believe we can get through anything.

"It has. I'm having a hard time adjusting to not being able to touch you as much. I love our cuddles. And if I'm totally honest, I'm struggling with knowing that you are growing a child that isn't for us to keep," I admit.

"But we agreed. You said you didn't want to be a parent." Quent looks genuinely shocked and horrified.

Their eyes widen and their chin wobbles like they might cry. The urge to comfort them is overpowering, and my heart clenches at making them sad. This is the reason I've allowed us to put off the conversations we need to be having, but no more. Even if it hurts, better to let the hurt out than keep it bottled up where it can only fester.

"I did." I incline my head toward them and stretch out my legs in front of me. "But I also never expected you to carry a child when we discussed that. I still don't necessarily want to be a parent, but I want to be involved with any kid you bring into this world."

"We will." Quent grips my wrist, more gently than before, slipping their fingers around my palm. They squeeze until I meet their gaze. "Jared promised. And you know I was over there all the time when they had Thomas. Ira won't be any different."

"Ira?" I repeat the name.

"Oh, yeah! They decided on a name. Told me at lunch. Isn't it cute?" Quent bounces in the suds, clearly pleased with the baby's name. "They wanted something gender neutral."

"That is cute." I smile. Ira. I can picture a tiny version of Quent with that name. "I'm excited to meet Ira."

"Me too. Sooo excited! I want to go back to being okay with my body again. But I am kind of excited to feel the goober kicking soon. I'll be mad if I can't see teeny tiny hands and feet trying to protrude through my abdomen."

That makes me chuckle. "I'm not sure if it works quite the way you're imagining, pup."

Quent shrugs. "I saw it on the internet, so it must be true." They blow bubbles in the water, as if that's the final word on the matter. I drop it in favor of watching them splash around for a while.

"You'll keep talking to me about what you need?" I ask after a comfortable silence filled with them splashing and humming a song to themself.

"Yep. Need you." They flash me a suggestive smile. "Want to join me to rinse off?"

"Sure." I strip to join them as they drain the tub and turn on the shower to rinse away the bubbles.

"Can I taste you?" Q kneels in front of me with pleading eyes when I step into the tub. "Need to make you feel good."

"Whatever you want is yours, puppy." I tousle their hair.

"I want you." Q licks their lips and places their hands on my thighs, urging me to open for them. "It hurts that I can't give all of myself to you like I usually do, but I still need to be close to you in the ways I can. I love you, Mommy. And I miss you."

"I've missed you too, baby. We'll figure this out. I don't need anything you aren't comfortable giving me." I cut my gaze toward the lacy something in the trash. "As long as we keep talking, we'll figure out how we can make this work." It's a promise I know we both mean.

"That goes both ways," Q observes. They lick their lips. "I get that you don't like to burden me, but I know you'd have volunteered to be the one doing this if you could. You can talk to me about it if you're struggling."

"You're right. It's hard. And I don't want to make this harder for you, but if it was an option, I think I'd want to carry our kids." I press a fist against my abdomen, to ease the dull ache of longing for something that can never be at the idea of growing one of Q's eggs inside of me. I'd have done it if I had a uterus. What I'm less sure about is whether I could handle giving a baby I carried to Jared and Logan to raise. Not if I looked down into eyes that match Q's, so earnest and full of trust in me. I shake my head to clear away that fantasy.

"Ours?" Q turns watery eyes on me, looking on the verge of tears. "You'd want that?"

I hesitate to answer. Part of me does want that. Perhaps in another life, if I'd fallen in love with someone who wanted to be a parent with me, that's a path I'd have chosen. But Quent doesn't want kids of our own, and I want them more than any hypothetical future child.

When I consider all the people I have in my life to mother, I realize that I don't need a child to fulfill that part of me. Between nurturing our friends when they need me and being Q's Mommy, I am as much a mother as I need to be. I can be a doting aunt to the child Quent is carrying, and any siblings that come along for them, through surrogacy or any other means. I don't need to carry a child to feed that part of myself..

"I'm sorry." Q hunches their shoulders, their voice is watery with unshed tears.

"It's not your fault." I pat their back to console them. "I think this is something I needed to deal with. Being a Mommy matters to me. It's a huge part of me. And while I don't need to experience a pregnancy for that to be true, it's still something I need to mourn. That doesn't change the fact you are more than enough for me, Quentin. Don't you ever believe any differently."

"Okay. I love you, Mommy. I hate making you feel sad."

"You aren't." I put all my conviction into my voice. "This situation is hard for both of us, but I'm still proud of what you are doing for your brother."

"It's for all of us, really. We're going to have the best nibling. I want to see you be their aunt as much as I want Jared to be a dad. And at least the pregnancy and all the messy feels that come with it for both of us is temporary, right?" They need me to reassure them, so I do.

Even though there are parts of this that are hurting me too, it's a relief to share some of the burden with my partner. There are times when I can't be the strong one who shoulders all our burdens alone. Times when I owe it to Quent to share the load with them as my equal, and tonight is one of those times. We need each other.

"Right." I nod decisively, and their answering smile lights their face. After this conversation, I believe that we'll get through this. My emotions aren't just a burden for me to keep from them, and they see me as clearly as I see them.

"And once the baby is here, we can see if being an aunty is enough for you, or if we want something more?" Quent bites their lip nervously. My stomach swoops at the enormity of what they're potentially offering. They're willing to consider something so monumental if it's something I need. It's reassuring to hear that they are as committed to meeting my needs as I am to them and theirs. That alone means more to me than the offer itself.

"We can." I smile at them, hoping they can see all the love in my eyes.

"Can I love on you now?" Quent reaches for me.

"Yes." I settle their hands on my hips.

They lick a tentative stripe over my groin, then eat me out like they're starving for pussy and can't get enough of me. Which is fitting, since I can't get enough of them, either. I throw my head back and let the pleasure wash over me in waves.

There's so much Quent is saying with this simple act. That they're sorry for the distance between us lately, even though I never really blamed them as much as the situation. That it doesn't mean they don't want me just as much as ever, even when they're struggling with their body right now.

They're showing me I'm loved and appreciated just as much as I love them. Quent is taking care of me the best way they know how, and that means the world. It makes the physical sensations almost secondary to the certainty that we'll get through this pregnancy together, no matter how hard things get.

I have to lean against the wall, hands curled in their hair to steady myself by the time they make me come with their talented tongue on my clit. Q keeps their lips sealed around me through the full body orgasm, their mouth hot on my sensitive flesh. I cradle them close, hoping to convey all my boundless love for them as they make love to me. When it's over, they gaze up at me with longing, and I pull them up to stand in front of me.

"Your turn. Show me how you want me to stroke your cute little cock, Quentin."

Q presses their back to my front and lets me hold them in the warm water. They guide my hands to where they are comfortable being touched. Wrap my fingers around their junk and guide me through jerking them off while the water runs over us both.

When they sag against me afterward, I turn off the water and get us both dried and bundled into bed. Uncharacteristically, they insist on wearing a loose t-shirt to cover up. I need to get used to that new normal. But despite their newly kindled insecurities about their body, tonight, they snuggle close to me for comfort in their sleep. Still my sweet cuddle-monster trusting me to take care of them, come what may.

CHAPTER 13
Quent

"Here's what we're going to do." Mommy props her elbows on the table. She leans toward me, taking both my hands in hers. It's been a few days since the ultrasound and my failed attempt to embrace the changes to my body that only made my dysphoria worse.

"Hmm? Do?" I look up from my soggy bowl of cereal, wondering what I missed while I was zoning out. "Do about what?"

"You've been avoiding your friends." Mommy squeezes my hands.

"Na uh. We went to the Summer Fling. I even made a new friend," I counter.

"That was a few weeks ago. Have you called Bobby about actually getting together?" Mommy asks.

"Yeah. We've got D&D this weekend."

"Which you were talking about skipping this week."

"We haven't deep-cleaned the playroom since the last play party." I refuse to meet her eyes because we both know I'm making excuses. "This weekend would be a good time to do it before I get as big as a house and can't help as much."

"You're avoiding people."

"I had Connor over last week." I realize too late that I've made her case for her. Too bad Jared got all the slippery lawyer genes. I decide to blame him for losing this argument. And for us having it in the first place, since it's his kid I'm carrying.

"You did." Mommy nods. "And coincidentally, he's the only one you've told about the bun in your oven."

"So?" I pout out my lip like a petulant child.

"So, we're going to invite your friends over for a playdate, and you're going to tell them all about our future nibling."

"I *could* do that. Or..." I draw out the single syllable far longer than is reasonable. "We could just have my friends over for a play date and *not* tell them." The panicky flutter in my chest at the thought of this changing things with my closest friends makes that seem like an excellent idea even though I know better. "We've had to have our D&D sessions at Harry's all summer with the club closed, so it might be fun to meet up here just to hang out for once."

"Weren't you planning to meet up with Martin's new boy at Adventures for your next gaming session?"

"Yeah." I hunch my shoulders, because she's right, but I really want to hide from this announcement. It's silly, but emotions never bothered with logic.

Connor has known about the whole surrogacy thing since the day I made my impulsive offer. So it was natural to text him with my positive test as soon as I got home from work that first day. Telling the rest of our friends is harder. Or more stressful, rather.

Monty, Tate, and Harry have never given me a reason to think they see me as anything other than who I am. But it's still intimidating to tell them I'm knocked up when that's such a femme-coded state of being. It's so ingrained in everything to do with pregnancy that it's been making me uncomfortable and restless to think about other people knowing.

When we went shopping, I found some cool surrogacy shirts with storks on them online. I'm as ready as possible for the dreaded day when I can't hide my belly under baggy layers anymore and it misgenders me for all the world to see.

On the bright side, the shirts helped me decide I want to be called stork instead of aunt or uncle. I never settled on a title that fit when I was hanging out with Thomas before he went back to his mom.

Mommy lifts my hands to her face and kisses the back of each of them. "Puppy, at some point, they are going to find out about the baby. Unless you're planning some sort of cloistering once your belly is too big to hide?"

I giggle at the thought of retiring to some country estate to languish away the final trimester. Connor's family might actually let me stay with them for a while. His folks have a big old farmhouse in the countryside with several guest rooms now that most of their brood has left the nest.

"You're actually planning it, aren't you?" Mommy correctly reads my expression.

"Um, no? Shifty eyes. Just hear me out though. We could stay with Con's folks. Go to all Marietta's soccer games, help with the twins' after-school activities and babysit Connor's niblings. Plus, with him rearranging his work schedule to spend his weekends with them twice a month, I'd probably get to see him bunches if we stayed with his folks. And you can work from anywhere."

Mommy lets go of my hands and cups my face between her palms. Her touch is warm and grounding. "Monty, Harry, and Tate won't look at you differently because you opted to make use of your uterus, Quentin. None of our close friends will."

"Yeah, but what if they do?" I whine. That's better than facing the fear of learning something about people I love that I can't unlearn. I don't think I will. It would honestly shock me, but the shadow of doubt is hard to stomp out without actually telling them.

Mommy sighs and strokes my cheek. "Then that goes to show they aren't someone you can trust with all of yourself and it's a valuable thing to know. I won't blow smoke. There are people who won't get it or who might say hurtful things to you. But if you honestly think your closest friends won't accept your choices about your body, you might need to reevaluate those friendships."

"I don't want to lose them." And the more people who know, the more people are going to find out. While my close friends are almost definitely going to follow my lead on how to react to the news, I have no illusions that strangers will be universally accepting.

"And if they're worth keeping around, you won't. Granted, I'm not entirely opposed to spending some time in the countryside as a vacation if you need a break from being around people. However, it might be better to stay close to the doctors we trust until this kid is out of you, no?"

"Yeah. You're right." I shudder at the thought of delivering this baby in a strange hospital with some carbon copy of one of the sneering doctors of my youth. The ones who refused to listen to me about my hypothyroid symptoms. Let alone those who rebuffed my first fumbling attempts to get on T, before that. No, thank you. Besides, I want Jared and Logan to be close by once their kid is here. I want to see them hold their baby for the first time. I should ask Jax to take newborn photos. That would be the sort of memory I want to preserve.

"About staying in the city or telling our friends?"

"Both. We can start with my gaming group, since Connor already knows, anyway."

"And our pup group?"

"Didn't you tell Clark and Nicholas that it took?"

"I did. But that's not the entire group," Mommy says.

I roll my eyes. "Are you forgetting that Nicholas is an incorrigible gossip? Unless you specifically told him it's a secret, he would have told Ethan at a minimum. And more likely he told every pup at the mosh because it didn't occur to him not to mention the hot scene we did."

"Is it a secret?" Mommy arches a brow at me.

"Not really." I sigh. "I'd honestly rather have Niko tell everyone than have to make some sort of weird announcement. So long as no one gets the idea that it's Niko's kid. Nicholas and Clark are the ones I'm closest to in that group anyway, and since they participated in the process, I doubt they have an issue with it."

Mommy barks out a laugh. "Quite the contrary." Her smile softens to something borderline seductive. "Clark tells me Niko is quite eager for a repeat performance."

I assume my most flirtatious tone. "Do you want to watch me getting serviced by his big fat knot again, Mommy?"

"I want you panting and desperate for it. Next time you'll have to show us how good you are with that mouth before you get a fat juicy cock anywhere near that breedable little hole of yours. You were devastatingly hot that night, desperate and begging for my permission."

My breathing is a little ragged just remembering the scene. "So, uh, you'll arrange another playdate for him to breed me? I know I said I'm feeling weird about my junk, but that still sounds hot."

"I will." Mommy tips my chin up for a sweet kiss. "After you tell your other friends about the baby."

"Fine." I pout, but it seems like a pretty fair deal to me. "I'll have them over for a movie night before our session with Bobby at Adventures. We can order in and I'll tell them all."

"That's my brave pup." Mommy gives me a perfunctory peck on the lips.

"So, you should totally set up that playdate with Clark."

"I'll call him and see about getting the jumbo bottle of cum lube to shoot you full of pretend spunk. Pretty sure he's been playing with Niko and Ethan as a pair recently, so you could get two studs this time. We'll let them take turns making you a sloppy mess for me. Two big, strong alphas stuffing you full of their jizz. How does that sound?"

"Mm. Yes, please. Double the fun." I can practically feel the heated rush of fluids and the ache of the cum-shooting toy's knot stretching me to my limits as Niko thrusts into me with frantic urgency. The bruising press of his paw mitts biting into my flanks to pin me in place, the rawness of the coupling. Both our handlers' eyes glued on us, drinking in the sight of us together.

I hope Mommy will let me bury my face in her folds again afterward. I love tasting her while she grips my collar just hard enough to remind me it's there, and she owns me. Half the fun was in knowing it was her will that had me pinioned under the big stud. Her desire to watch me getting bred so deep a piece of that encounter is still growing inside me made the encounter all the sweeter. I love the power of giving her that kind of control over me. Her deciding when and how it will happen.

For a repeat of that night, I can handle telling my best friends about my future nibling. I just hope it doesn't change anything between us.

**

The promised movie night is anticlimactic. I put on one of my new stork shirts to greet my friends, hoping that it will do most of the telling for me.

"Oh, so you're announcing it?" Connor asks, pointing to the graphic over my barely there bump as he and Jax enter the house before the others arrive.

"Yep." I nod.

"I was wondering why the spur of the moment get-together right before game night. Monty is sure you have some juicy gossip to dish about Bobby before we hang with him."

"Nope. I mean, unless you count the fact I saw Martin bringing the sounding kit from the medical room home." I wiggle my eyebrows at Connor and he grins.

Martin wasn't trying to hide the toy when I saw it, so I figure it's okay to share. Half the club was there to see him with it last week after the Fling. And Bobby was eyeing it the way I watch my favorite toys. Or cheesy fries when my nibling isn't being a monster and tricking my brain into thinking banana sandwiches sound more delicious than foods I actually like. They don't sound good. Except, right now, they kind of sound amazing. Even more so with some Nutella and jam. I don't even like bananas, and yet here we are. I rub at my belly, as though that might quell the kid's terrible ideas.

"Ooh, sounds like Bobby is a lucky boy." Connor grins conspiratorially, drawing my attention back to him.

Jax slings an arm around Connor's waist and draws him close to kiss his cheek. "Say the word, Conman. You, too, can be a lucky boy."

"I'm already a lucky boy." Connor gives Jax a look I've never seen him use on anybody before. Bedroom eyes. I knew those two would hit it off. Their budding relationship fills me with smug self-satisfaction. Connor deserves to be loved.

"Behave." Jax gives Connor's ass a gentle swat, then kisses his cheek. "Kylee mentioned mocktails?"

"Yep. She's got a pitcher on the back patio." I nod sagely. Okay, enough hanging out in the entryway. I grab Connor's hand and lead him toward the den where I've got the movie ready to go. "Littles in the den, bigs out back."

"Thanks." Jax heads to the sliding door.

"Come on, I need to make a thing." I drag Connor to the kitchen to make that sandwich I suddenly need with the fiery passion of a tiny mini-human directing my life. Weird, but at least it isn't pickles and ice cream. For now. Connor hitches a hip against the counters and watches me rummage around for what I need.

"Pretty sure you're already making a thing." He tips his head toward my midsection with a teasing smirk. That's when I discover the Nutella jar only contains a few scrapings and have to hunt through the cupboard for the backup jar I'm sure has to be here. Or else.

"Not a thing. A precious tiny tyrant who demands to be fed gross things."

"Ah. Cravings? My sister dipped nachos in mixed berry yogurt until they got all soggy when she was pregnant the first time. Can't stand to eat nachos ever since."

"Yeah. I don't know why, but bananas sound fantastic right now." I rub at my belly.

"You like bananas though." Connor points out.

"No. I like *talking about* bananas. I don't actually like eating them. They're too mushy. And slimy and eurgh." I shudder theatrically.

"But you need a banana sandwich right this second or you'll bite someone?" Connor is obviously trying to suppress his amusement at my gross craving predicament.

"Pretty much sums it up..." I climb up on the counter to check the top shelf and whoop in triumph as I find my prize. "Score! I knew Mommy bought more." The doorbell rings, which means I probably missed someone knocking and now Mommy might come to get it. I hastily cradle the jar to my chest and spin to hop down from the counter before I get caught breaking the rules.

"Don't fall, Q." Connor gives me a concerned look.

I scowl at him. "I'm not breakable."

"No, but all the changes can throw off your balance. No need to take silly risks." He gestures vaguely to my more pronounced curves. I shudder at the attention. His recognition that my body is changing doesn't make me any less grumpy. I set down the Nutella and cross my arms over my chest as I turn away from him so I don't snap or burst into tears over practically nothing.

The sliding door opens, so that means Mommy is answering the door and I'm free to stay here and finish making my snack. In my periphery, I see Connor approaching me.

"You okay in here?" Mommy asks, pausing in the doorway.

"Yeah," I answer reflexively. Except that's not true and I don't lie to Mommy. "I will be. Hormones." I force a wry laugh. Mommy hesitates.

"I've got them." Connor wraps his arms around me from behind and hooks his chin over my shoulder. "Hey, sorry, Q. I didn't mean to upset you."

"You didn't. It's just this is getting to the part where it's noticeable. I can't bind and I don't like it." It's easier to admit all that after discussing things with Mommy the other day. Like that conversation smashed the dam holding back all my messy emotions, so I no longer need to bottle them up inside.

Connor hugs me tighter, careful to avoid the curvy bits that are at the root of my moodiness, and rocks me from side to side. "Want me to get your robe or a blanket from the den so you can cocoon in it while I make your sandwich?"

I nod, my eyes all teary from him caring. "Yes, please." I sniffle.

"It'll be okay, Q." Connor brushes his lips against my cheek.

"Yeah." I grip his hands to keep him from pulling away from me.

"The others are going to follow your lead about this whole thing, if that's part of why you're feeling raw tonight."

I nod again.

Connor doesn't pull away. "I've got you, Q."

I lean back into him for a moment longer. Monty's overly excited voice drifts in from the entryway. Luke is with him, and Tate, judging from the number of voices chatting with Mommy. I take a deep breath and step free of Connor's embrace.

"You okay?" he asks.

"Yeah. Blanket me!" I demand imperiously. Connor steps back and snaps me a mock salute.

"As you wish." He jogs into the den and gathers up a wearable blanket from the tangle of soft stuff I dumped there to make a snuggle nest later. He brings the bright blue fleece to me and holds it up for me to stick my arms in the sleeves. Then Connor wraps the voluminous fabric around me and guides me to sit in one of the kitchen chairs.

"Thanks, Con." I smile at him.

"Don't mention it. Now, tell me what manner of culinary abomination I am committing here." He rolls up his sleeves and flashes me a dimpled grin. I direct him to make the sandwich I'm envisioning. Nutella, banana sliced lengthwise, thinly sliced onion and a bit of lettuce for crunch.

"Okay, now the real question, cut into triangles, or are you truly an unredeemable kitchen gremlin?"

I stick my tongue out at him. "Rectangles."

Connor blows a raspberry at me and cuts the sandwich neatly in half. "I'd say you ruined it, but I think your ingredient choice pre-ruined it," he jokes, setting the plate in front of me just as our friends join us in the kitchen.

"Hey, Q." Monty bounds over to me and pokes at my food. "Whatcha got there?"

"A banana sandwich." I open it up to show him. Monty makes a face.

"Um, is that what you meant when you said we'd have dinner here?" he asks with poorly disguised disgust.

I laugh at his expression. "No. This is my special puppy chow. Want some?" I wave the sandwich toward him.

"Ew. No. That's gross." Monty holds up his hands to fend off the sandwich. I take a big bite just to further provoke his reaction.

"What did we say about calling other people's food gross?" Luke arches a brow at Monty.

Monty turns toward Luke, thinks better of whatever protest he was about to make. He pouts and then turns back toward me. "Sorry, Q. I'm sure your weird food tastes fine to you."

Tate snorts at the fail apology. I can't hide my smile at that. "It does, thanks."

"So, are you, like, pregnant or something?" Monty asks with another dubious look at my sandwich. "Because like...onions and chocolate on a sandwich are totally on par with the classic pickles and ice cream stereotype."

"And you got all green and gagged when I offered you cheese fries at the munch last month…" Tate chimes in.

Monty frowns, glances at my blanket swaddled body, considers my face and then grins at me. "You are, aren't you?" He turns his big goofy grin toward Mommy and then back to me. I muster up a return smile, even though my guts are roiling with nerves. I set down my sandwich, appetite gone.

"It's not like that. I'm a surrogate. For Jared and Logan," I explain.

"Ah. So, you're finally getting a nibling?" Tate asks. He's smiling too.

"That's the plan. Should hand the little goblin to their parents around February." I hold my breath for their response to the news. Monty squeaks excitedly and gloms onto me in a big hug that would have knocked my sandwich from my hands if I were still holding it.

"That's awesome, Q. Congrats." Monty claps me on the back, then steps aside.

The others offer more subdued congratulations. Mommy watches me closely, assessing if I need her to swoop in and give me some time to get myself under control, but I'm good. She was right about my friends taking the news in stride. I give her a subtle head shake. I'm okay now that they know and they aren't reacting badly. More than okay, it's a weight off my shoulders that I wasn't consciously aware of carrying.

Mommy pats me on the back, rubbing between my shoulders before leading Rory and Luke outside with her to rejoin Jax on the back patio. That leaves me alone with Connor, Monty, Tate, and Harry. They all seem to pick up that I'm not my usual bubbly self.

Harry's the one who breaks the awkward silence. "So, how are you doing?"

"Sicker than I expected at first. That's mostly let up now that I'm in the second trimester and I've got my thyroid levels where they need to be." I take a hearty bite of my sandwich.

"Did you mean to tell us, yet?" Tate asks.

"Yeah, I planned to tell you all tonight. Before it got too obvious. I got a fun shirt for the occasion and everything."

"Let's see?" Monty asks. I struggle free of my blanket swaddle and show him the stork printed on my belly. "Nice. Just the stork, not the mama." He reads off the slogan. "I wonder if they make shirts with Baby Sinclair saying 'not the mama' from *Dinosaurs*? I'd totally get you one of those."

"You would." I laugh. Monty has made us all watch that show on multiple occasions.

"I bet if they don't already sell it, we can get it made custom at one of those quick print places," Tate suggests. Monty pulls out his phone, no doubt searching for said t-shirt.

"Can we though? Isn't it a trademarked character or something?" Connor asks.

"I bet the custom shirt place on Granville would do it. They're pretty much willing to print anything." Harry chimes in. "They gave me a great deal on company polos a while back. Didn't even make me prove I owned the rights to my logo."

"No need, I found it. He's even holding up a frying pan. What size, Q?" He turns the phone to show me the shirt in question.

I laugh at the bald baby dinosaur puppet brandishing a frying pan. "Okay, you got me. I would totally wear that." I select my size from the dropdown menu when he continues to hold the phone in my face. "You don't have to get it for me though."

"Consider it a congrats on being preggers present. Those are a thing, right?" Monty adds it to his cart and places the order. "Are you having a shower or something?"

"No way." I shut that idea down fast. "There wouldn't be a point since I won't need baby stuff. I mean, beyond some extra stuff for when the kid visits."

"Are we throwing a shower for your brother and Logan, then?" Tate suggests.

"I don't think so?" I tug my collar to ground myself against the rising panic at being put on display for all my brother and Logan's coworkers and acquaintances. Definitely not doing that. "I don't know what they're planning. If they do something, I don't think I'd go. The focus should be on them and the baby. And I don't want that kind of attention on my body, you know? Plus, they have most of the baby gear from Thomas. I think they'll probably do some sort of welcome home baby party after the birth?"

"Cool." Monty nods.

"So, this doesn't change anything?" I ask, even though I'm pretty sure their reaction says it all.

"Uh, no? Should it?" Monty elbows me.

"No." I nudge him back.

"Did you think we'd care?" Tate's brow is all wrinkled in concern.

I give him a sheepish smile. "Kind of? It's more that I was afraid it would change how you see me."

"Nope. That's not gonna happen. Come here, you." Monty gloms onto me, squeezing me in a bearhug and grabbing at Tate to get him in on the action too. "Group hug!" he declares, waving Harry and Connor into the action.

All four of them squeeze me, patting my back, rubbing my hair and generally loving on me since they all know how much I love to be touched. I lean into it, content to be the center of this attention for as long as they want to give it. Their affection is a soothing balm that helps my lingering worries evaporate. All of them crushing me in between them like nothing has changed makes it easier to ignore the squirmy discomfort of my chest while we embrace.

"Um, guys?" Connor comments after a couple of long moments have passed. "The bigs are looking at us."

Sure enough, Jax is snapping photos of us through the sliding door and Mommy looks ready to come check on us. I wave, which dislodges Harry. The others all step back.

"They think we're up to something," Tate observes. He gives his Daddy a cheeky wave.

"Orgy?" I joke, leaning in to lick a stripe up Monty's cheek.

"Name the time and place," Monty teases back. It's not like we haven't fooled around before. And we probably will again. But him finding a partner might change how that looks for us.

"Uh, huh, and your Daddy wouldn't have anything to say about that?" I arch a brow at him.

Monty gives me a sheepish look. "Yeah, guess I need permission now." His beaming grin as he says it makes his feelings on that new necessity clear. "And I think I'm only allowed to do oral with other people."

"That's not a problem for me," I assure him, licking my lips.

"You two are such horndogs, save the sex talk for a play party." Connor shoves at Monty's shoulder and he lets go of me, the last to break the hug.

"Are we still ordering food?" Monty asks, his eyes darting

dubiously to my abandoned sandwich. I grab it for another bite. The flavors shouldn't go together, but I can't help a happy moan as I chew.

"Yeah," I mumble through a full mouth.

"Good, because I'm famished. Here are our options." Connor grabs the stack of paper menus for Mommy and my favorite local delivery options from in the drawer by the fridge. He sorts through the stack, removing several that lack kosher options for him and one that only does fried diner fare that I haven't been able to stomach for months.

We pick a restaurant and collect orders from our partners before placing the order. And then we get down to some serious binge-watching in the den. I brought up the bean bag chairs from the basement for the five of us to lounge on. That along with most of the blankets I own forms the perfect base for a huge cuddle pile. It takes some squirming and shuffling for all of us to get comfy. Once we settle in, I love having them all close by and touching me as our first movie of the marathon streams.

I rest my head in Connor's lap and he scratches my scalp. Monty tucks an arm around me, letting me mold myself against his soft belly. Tate's head is resting next to my belly on Monty's other side. Harry sits by my feet, and as he gets more comfortable with how physically affectionate all of us are, he rubs at my ankles. Encouraged, I put my feet in his lap. He takes the hint and massages them, making me sigh happily.

"You look comfy," Mommy comments when the doorbell rings for our food delivery. "Want us to serve you lot?"

"That's what bigs are for," I agree cheekily. The comment gets me a warning look and I flash her my sweetest most innocent smile. "Please?"

"Is Monty's brattiness rubbing off on Q?" Luke teases.

"Monty can rub off on me anytime," I shoot back with a wink.

I wriggle my ass against him. Monty swats it. "Stop talking, I haven't seen this one before."

"Ow," I whine, rubbing at the spot he hit, even though it barely stings at all. "What kind of monster spanks a preggo?" I appeal to Connor. He puts a finger over my lips to shush me. I bite at it ineffectually.

"That's what you get for being a brat." Monty snuggles me closer and pins me against his body so I can't squirm as much. "I should know."

I stifle a laugh at that. "You like it," I remind him.

"Very much. Now either pause the movie or be quiet."

"Pause it." Mommy sets two enormous bags of food on TV trays to sort through everyone's orders.

Harry hits the pause button while Mommy and Luke distribute the food. We all shuffle around enough so that we're upright for eating. Rory and Jax bring a selection of drinks, which they pour into sippy cups for Tate, Connor, and Monty. Harry and I get straws. Once we're all served, the bigs settle in on the couch to watch the rest of the movie with us. Harry hits play and we resume our movie night, going back to a giant cuddle pile as soon as we consume the food.

Only it's even better now because Mommy rests her feet on me, idly stroking them along the curve of my belly. Just enough gentle pressure to get me all squirmy and beyond horny from the teasing. Or it could be the pregnancy hormones making me horny. Either way, I'm more than happy to retire to our room as soon as our last guest leaves.

CHAPTER 14

Quent

B y the final trimester, I am so ready to have this kid. I mean. I don't want baby Ira to have any problems, so I'll tough it out for as long as the pregnancy lasts. But I wouldn't complain if she made her debut a few weeks early.

Jar likes to joke that if the kid is anything like her stork, she'll be fashionably late, but he can eat those words. With ketchup and mashed bananas. Hm, that sounds like a delicious sandwich. Perfect for midnight snacking. If only tomatoes, in all their forms, didn't give me awful indigestion now that my uterus is making a grab for the territory formerly held by my other internal organs.

I've already started mainlining raspberry tea. It's supposed to be a uterine tonic. Herbal tea and dates to soften my cervix and basically begging Mommy for as many orgasms as she'll give me each night after work. Though that part might not be much different from my norm. Except we have to get creative about positions to accommodate the changes in my body.

As to checking off every home remedy for hurrying along my labor, I've given serious consideration to borrowing some jizz from a friend. It's supposed to have prostaglandins that can help kick labor into gear. That request probably wouldn't be the weirdest thing I've asked of my closest friends. It certainly wouldn't be the first time I inspired them to orgasm. Plus, there is something poetic about ending this pregnancy the same way it started.

Not sure I want to go *quite* that far. But, when I'm up several times a night, rolling out of bed to stagger to the bathroom to pee—again—it's tempting. Add in feeling like an achy beached whale with no sense of balance, and yeah, part of me wants to consider it. Along with every other folk remedy that's out there.

We've tried long walks and spicy food. Sex. Nipple stimulation. That one should be fun, but I almost skipped it and I called it off after a few shuddery seconds. It still makes my insides go all squirmy in a bad way ever since the pregnancy hormones made my chest fill out. I'm still really hoping that's temporary. Not wanting her hands and lips on any part of me doesn't work for me. I want to get back to being able to give her all of me without reservations. So this kid can make her debut any time now.

At least genetics are on my side. My mother nursed Jared and I, and she was pretty much as flat as I've always been after weaning us off breastmilk. Much as I love my niece already, I don't think I'll be offering to pump for her. That was something we talked about as an option when this was all theoretical, but in practice I already know it's a big fat hell no. Fran offered to let me order Jared baby formula at cost through the pharmacy's wholesaler, though, so that's a pretty good consolation prize.

I rock from one butt-cheek to the other in the bed. Who knew I'd be fantasizing about sleeping flat on my belly again? I guess that's something the pregnancy bloggers might have mentioned, but it didn't seem like a big deal until I was stuck like this.

I groan, too tired to get up, despite the insistent pressure from my bladder. Mommy reaches over and rubs along my collar bones. The one area on my torso that won't get her head bitten off because I'm a hormonal mess.

"Gotta pee." I whine.

"Want me to get puppy pads so you can just go in the corner?" Mommy jokes. I know it's a joke because that's something from both of our no lists.

"Oh, I know. I could wear a diaper like Tate."

"I love you to the moon, puppy, but that is so not my kink."

"Would you change me if I needed it though?" I press, even though the idea of laying here in a wet diaper makes my skin itchy and only increases my urgent need for the washroom.

Mommy rolls over and kisses my nose. "I'd do anything for you, love." She sing-songs.

"But not that?" I pout, recognizing the tune of the song.

"For you? Even that. But seeing as how I can see you squirming at the thought, why don't I help you up so you can pee in the toilet instead?" She rolls out of bed and comes around to my side to offer me her hands.

"Yes, please." I grip both her wrists and Mommy helps lever me up to my feet. It shouldn't be this hard, but the rapid changes to my center of balance are a pain to adjust to. "Thanks, Mommy." I toddle off to take care of my business. Mommy follows, probably because I tripped over my own feet last night and almost fell. She's a worrier.

When I actually get to the washroom, I'm glad she came along, because there's blood in my pajamas. And that makes me freak the fuck out that something is wrong with Ira.

"Mommy?" I ask, holding up the stained toilet paper. "What do I do?" My voice squeaks up an octave and my hand shakes bad enough that I'm afraid I might drop the bloody paper. I can barely breathe past the dread and terror. I can't lose Ira now. Just no. I'm hyperventilating and my vision tunnels.

"Breathe." Mommy kneels beside me. She plucks away the

paper and drops it into the toilet. "Focus on me, baby." She takes my face between her hands and holds me steady, taking charge. "Breathe, nice and slow with me. All you need to do is breathe for now." My panic recedes enough to make eye contact and try to regulate my breathing to match her deep, steady breaths.

"Do you feel her kicking?" Mommy asks when I'm a little calmer.

That has the panic moving back into high gear as I try to remember the last time I noticed Ira moving. Was she kicking as much as usual today? I'm drawing a total blank. My doctor has an emergency line, but hell if I can remember the number. Should we just go to the hospital? Or Jared's place. Or…I don't know.

I poke and press at my belly with increasing urgency until Ira kicks me hard in retaliation. That settles some of my worry. The baby is still okay. Or at least okay enough to move around and rabbit kick my bladder as penance for disturbing her rest.

"What do we do?" I ask, desperation for this to turn out alright in my pleading whine.

"For now, you just breathe." Mommy tugs on my collar to ground me and it helps. I believe her when she says, "I've got you, pup." She presses her phone to her ear. A moment later, she makes an irritated sound and leaves a message with my name and her number, then sets the phone on the counter. "The prerecorded message says the on-call doc will get back to us as soon as possible."

"Bleeding is bad though, right?" I reach for her and she hugs me tight.

"It could be a sign of labor. Remember, we were reading about that?" Mommy massages the small of my back, easing the ache that's been building there for what seems like weeks now.

"Mm, that's nice."

"Your back hurts?"

"Yeah. I mean, it's been achy for a while now that I've got, like, fifteen pounds of baby pulling on it. But today's been worse, off and on."

"Hmm. Would you say the pain came in waves?"

"Yeah." I give her a puzzled look. "How'd you know?"

"Puppy, have you considered that you might be in labor?"

"I figured that was just wishful thinking. I mean, I'd know if it was actual contractions, right?"

"Right." Mommy nods sagely. "Because of your vast experience with labor."

I scowl and paw at her hands. "Stop being smug and rub my back. Your hands help."

Mommy turns me to face away and puts pressure on my lower back, the way they taught her to do during labor at our birthing class. "Why don't we try timing the aches?"

"Mm. Okay. Now." I nod, bracing against the wall and pressing back into her hands as the ache peaks. The high point seems to stay that way for an absolute age before ebbing. "How long was that?"

"About a minute."

"Ungh," I groan. "It seemed like forever."

"Do you have your bag all packed?"

"I was gonna do it tomorrow."

"Okay, I've got some quick packing to do, pup. Call Jared and Logan to come over, okay?"

"What if it's nothing though?" I get my pajamas pulled back into place.

"Then it's nothing and they can sleep in the guest room." Mommy pockets her phone and leads me back to our bed. She lays my travel bag on the coverlet and starts filling it with everything from the hospital go-bag checklists I've been browsing online.

"You really think I'm in labor?" I ask, and despite being desperate for this day for weeks, now that it's a possibility, I'm anxious as hell about it. I put both hands on my belly and jiggle it around. The thump as Ira kicks again is a reassurance.

So many things could go wrong. And it's going to be messy and painful and I really just want to skip to the good part.

The sleepy newborn wrapped in a soft blanket and surrounded by all the people I love. All the people who love her.

Another surge in the pain breaks me out of my fantasies about skipping the actual delivery part of this endeavor.

"Mommy?" I call to her and she tosses the pair of slippers she is holding toward the bag and comes to my side.

"Another one?" Mommy confirms.

I nod miserably, sliding off the bed to curl around my belly. I turn to present Mommy with my back in a silent plea for her to make it better. She does—as much as she can, her hands help. Her touch always makes everything better. I whine until it turns into a moan and the lower sound helps center me so I can ride out the ache.

"That's it puppy, like taking a flogging; you can handle it." Mommy soothes. I want to snarl at her, but she's right. The same techniques that let me take as much fun pain as she wants to dish out can help with this less than fun version. Fun being a relative term, I am far from a pain slut at my best. This wave seems to stretch longer than the last.

"How long?" I pant when I can form coherent words.

"Bit over a minute. And less than five minutes apart. I think we might want to meet your brother at the hospital, okay?"

"The doctor said to call when it's ten minutes apart."

"Yep."

"So…this is happening?" I crawl up to sit on the bed again,

"Yeah, I think it's go time." Mommy leans in for a kiss. "You've got this, Q. You're the strongest pup I know and you'll get through this and soon we'll get to meet Ira in person, okay?"

I nod. "Yeah. Okay. Can you grab towels for the car? In case…"

"On it." Mommy tips my chin up for one more kiss. I hobble down the hall.

Mommy takes my arm to steady me on the stairs. I accept her help without a word since my balance is even more screwy with the dull ache in my back and the threat of another contraction looming.

She helps me out to the car, pausing to provide me with counterpressure through another contraction along the way. Okay, so shit is getting real.

Once I'm safely ensconced in the front seat, I buckle up and hit the button to call Jared. Mommy runs back inside to grab our stuff. I don't want her to go, but I can't deny it's necessary.

"'lo?" Jared's half-asleep confusion makes me irrationally ragey as another wave of pain grips me.

"I hate you, and your daughter is a menace." I moan into the phone.

"Quent?" Jared's voice goes from muzzy to alarmed. "Is everything okay?"

"No!" I wail into the phone. I'm dimly aware of Logan's voice in the background of the call. I whine into the phone and try to find some escape from the pain. There isn't one, so I just cling to the car's oh shit bar and try to ride out the contraction, ignoring Jared's increasingly alarmed questions.

When I think I can't take anymore, Mommy returns to the car. She sounds winded, but her concerned voice murmuring reassurances breaks through the fog of pain. Her soothing hands don't help as much this time. The angle is wrong with her leaning across the console beside me. And the car is uncomfortable and I just want this baby out right the fuck now.

"Just breathe, puppy, I've got you. Breathe." Mommy tries to soothe me. I dig my nails into my palms. The sharp sting distracts from the mounting ache and my irritation at everyone around me. The contraction ends. I unclench and flop back in my seat, panting with effort.

"Bad one?" Mommy asks when I've got it under control.

"Hospital!" I demand. Mommy puts the car in gear.

Jared and Logan are still on speaker. The sounds of them getting dressed come over the line. Dresser drawers thumping shut, rustling fabric and a zipper closing. I want them to shut up and let me just do this stupid thing already. Ira doesn't seem any happier about the developments than I am; a volley of retaliatory kicks knock against my ribs now that my organs have granted us both a temporary reprieve.

I rub a hand over my bump in a soothing gesture. The pang of loss at realizing I won't have it for much longer takes me by surprise. This is the moment I've looked forward to for weeks now.

I don't particularly enjoy being pregnant. I won't miss the constant misgendering, uninvited touches, frequent medical appointments, weird looks, inappropriate comments, or invasive questions. But there's something super cool about watching Ira do somersaults under my skin and knowing that my body is doing something miraculous.

"Hey, Jared, it's Kylee. Quent can't talk right now. They and Ira are both doing great, but the contractions are about three minutes apart. So if you guys want to head to the hospital, I think you'll be meeting your daughter shortly."

"We're on our way." Jared and Logan chorus. And then there's dead air. Until Mommy's phone rings and she sends the call to the car's bluetooth.

I tune out the backup doctor's voice as I curl around another contraction. The fucking seatbelt means I can't really move to alleviate the pain. It hurts worse than ever, though I'm not sure if that's because of my restricted position or if it's actually more intense. I let out some unholy sounds, cursing Jared, Logan, and the stupid impulse that got me into this position.

Mommy reaches for me, but I bat her hand away, snarling at her to drive faster. I don't want to be touched anymore. She gets the message and backs off. The car accelerates. I moan and rock in my seat, seeking any relief I can get.

"No, I don't think they can talk through the contractions at this point. And they're only a couple of minutes apart now." Mommy is saying when I'm in any position to pay attention to words again.

Mommy relays all my symptoms. The doctor agrees to meet us in labor and delivery with some hollow reassurances that, if my water hasn't broken yet, we probably still have more time than we think.

As soon as she hangs up, I feel a dull pop and hot liquid floods the towel under me.

"Well, fuck," I grumble. Mommy squeezes my hand. "So much for that line about my water not breaking yet."

"Almost there; hang on a little longer, pup."

Another wave of pain drowns out my response.

By the time we get to the hospital, all I want to do is push. I didn't get what people meant when they talked about that online, but it reminds me of having to take a massive dump. I just want what's inside me to be outside. Now. Right this fucking minute.

Mommy parks the car in the ER lot and takes my arm to lead me past the triage area and up to the gated entry to the obstetrics ward. She presses a buzzer and someone must have known to expect us, because they let us right inside. I figure that means I'll get to do my thing, but that isn't the case. They've got paperwork for me.

"We just need you to fill this out and then the doctor can assess you."

"You're joking." I throw the pencil. Mommy rescues the stack of paper before I can show them exactly what I think of their paperwork. The next contraction hits and I lean against the counter and give in to the urge to push. And the dull, thundering ache of the contractions is nothing compared to this novel sensation of burning fire ripping me open. It's like figging, only worse because I know that won't do any lasting damage and whatever this is aches as though it's going to tear me apart.

Someone is yelling something at me, but my wails drown out the noise. And then Mommy stands between me and my harassers until the contraction passes and the fire dulls to a raw burn. I imagine this might be what it's like to get anally fisted with zero prep. If the sadist doing the fisting opted for the warming lube.

"Hurts." I turn teary eyes to Mommy. She opens her arms for me. I turn my back on the nursing station and the paperwork to bury my face in her chest and squeeze tight.

"We need you to stop pushing until we get you in a room,

ma'am." Someone in scrubs chastises me.

"Fuck you!" I snarl.

"I don't think they can do that," Mommy interjects. Her presence anchors me. Makes this hell of pain and bright lights and demanding voices bearable. "Can we get them into a room and fill out the paperwork after?"

I cling to Mommy, trusting her to protect me until I need to push again. This time I at least know what to expect and the burn grows until it hits a peak and fades again. I still scream, and I'm pretty sure I need to take my soggy pants off before I can actually get Ira out.

As soon as the contraction passes, I shove my pants off. I've sure as hell been more naked in front of a bigger audience than this and the wet fabric is itchy and uncomfortable as well as being in the way.

"Whoa, wait a minute!" Someone tries to pull my pants back up, likely the same nurse who told me to hold in the baby. Whoever it is sounds very put out by my behavior. If Mommy didn't turn me away from them, I'd probably have kicked them in their stupid face. As it is, I step free of my sodden pants in time to squat down and push with the next contraction.

When it passes, they direct us into a room. I let Mommy shuffle me inside, but I'm not interested in my surroundings as long as she keeps holding me and keeps everyone else away.

There's a knock on the open door.

"Hi, Quent, how are we tonight?" I recognize the false-friendly voice of the on-call doctor from our clinic, and I growl at him.

He muffles a chuckle as he steps into the room, disinfecting his hands as he walks toward me. "Okay, wrong question, obviously. I guess we're doing this. Can I take a look?"

I grit my teeth and give him a sharp nod, just barely

remembering he won't recognize which of my whines means yes. I flinch at the gloved fingers touching my thighs as he squats down beside me. As he takes his look, the urge to push peaks again, along with another contraction.

"Alright, the baby is crowning. A few more big, strong pushes and the worst part will be over," he says.

I go limp in Mommy's arms as the contraction passes and rest against her chest.

"That's it, almost there." The doctor encourages me.

There's more talking. Nurses and other staff bustle around us, but I'm too busy pushing to care, as long as no one tries to make me move again. This time, the fire ebbs before the end of the contraction.

"That's it; can you give us two more big pushes?" The doctor encourages. I grunt and push again, and the fiery pressure goes away in a slick slide. The hands touching me go away too. All except for Mommy's arms around me.

Ira's first angry wail fills my ears, and I breathe a sigh of relief. I did it. It's over.

"That's it, you're doing fine, Quent. Just a few more pushes to deliver the placenta and you can rest."

I growl at the doctor's cheery instructions. Mommy's murmured sweet nothings ease me away from the brink of lashing out at him. As soon as it's actually over, the doctor prods at my nether regions. He declares them healthy before someone else slides weird mesh panties, already equipped with a huge absorbent pad, up my legs. I'm hustled unceremoniously into a bed.

I want to see Ira and ask if Jared and Logan are here yet, but I'm exhausted. Instead of worrying about the details, I let Mommy take care of all those other concerns and give in to the need to rest my eyes, just for a little while.

When I open them again, Jared is sitting in the chair next to my bed with Ira wrapped in a blanket on his chest. Logan and Mommy are standing nearby.

"Good morning," Mommy greets me. "Sleep well?"

"Yeah. How's Ira?"

"She's perfect, Q," Jared breathes, his eyes shiny with unshed tears. "She's so perfect."

"Apparently, I'm pretty good at crafting tiny humans," I joke.

"Humans, plural?" Jared teases me, a sparkle in his eyes.

I snort. "Ask me again when I'm not still bleeding from birthing your little watermelon. I swear she weighs at least twenty pounds."

"Six pounds, eight ounces of pure perfection," Logan corrects me. Typical lawyer, he always has to be right.

"Yeah, well, if you want to get your dick juice anywhere near my eggs again, you'll agree that she is the largest baby ever to be birthed here. Practically in the hospital lobby. And that I am a godlike entity for going through that for you guys."

"No arguments there." Logan holds his hands up in mock surrender. Jared laughs.

"Did you really growl at a nurse?" my brother asks.

"It was the doctor," I grumble. "If that nurse had tried to touch me, I can't vouch for whether I'd have bitten her though."

"That's my feisty little sib." Jared beams at me, pride evident in his tone. "You did so good, Q. You're our hero."

It warms me to my bones to know the loving adoration in his eyes is for me as much as it's for Ira and Logan.

"That's what family is for." I shrug it off. I'm not sure if I'm up to going through all of this again to help them give Ira a sibling, but I'm not ready to say never.

"And speaking of family, would you like to officially meet your niece?" Jared shifts Ira in his arms, like he's getting ready to offer her to me.

"Logan's held her?" I glance between the two of them.

Logan nods and smiles. "Gave her the first bottle and everything; she already eats like a champ. Just like the stork that brought her to us." He's teasing, so I stick out my tongue at him.

"Just wait until she's old enough for me to feed her the gross sandwich combinations she baby-telepathy-ed me into eating. Now give her to her stork." I reach for the baby and Jared carefully settles his blanket-wrapped bundle into my arms. Ira blinks wide blue eyes at me and smacks her sweet little bow lips.

That's when I know I'd do this a thousand times to have this moment right here. The pure perfection of cradling my niece's tiny warm body in my arms, breathing in her sweet baby scent. She's worth it. And so is the adoration in Mommy's eyes as she watches me holding Ira for the first time.

Kylee's smile when our eyes meet is worth every second of pain and dysphoria and all the strain the pregnancy piled on our relationship. Knowing that she was here for me means the world. She got me through the intense whirlwind that was labor and kept me safe when I was out of my head in pain among strangers.

She loves me enough to let go of Ira and smile at the niece I know a part of her wants to keep. The same way she smiles with genuine happiness when she shares the other parts of me. This woman is everything to me. My soul mate. I reach for her hand and Mommy stands beside me, clutching me tight as we gaze down at the baby in my arms together.

Ira nuzzles into my neck and sucks on my skin. "Aw, you're

a hungry little beastie," I joke, offering her a finger instead. Ira suckles, getting fussy when no food is forthcoming. Her grumpy newborn squawks are cute.

"On it!" Jared leans in to kiss my forehead. It's the same parental gesture from when I was having a hard time with my grief and living with him after our folks died. He's going to be such a good father to Ira. Heart full to bursting, I know I made the right call by doing this. Jared pats my hand. Then he's out the door to get his daughter's next meal.

Mommy steps closer to me, squeezing my shoulder and admiring the baby as I hold her. Ira is a warm weight on my chest. I love holding her, kissing her scalp full of wavy dark hair. The new baby smell of her is soothing, and I know I'm going to love her more with every passing day. It's almost enough to make me consider doing this again, but when Jared returns with the bottle, I'm perfectly happy to turn my niece over to her parents. Ira's the most perfect tiny human ever, but I still don't want to be a parent.

Watching Logan and Jared dote on their offspring makes me smile. And I'm perfectly content to let them bond with her while I rest and recover. Mommy doesn't let go of my hand, and that's all I really need.

Later, when I'm discharged and Mommy has paid the exorbitant fee for our little parking violation when we first arrived, she holds my hand over the console.

"So, how do you feel about all of this, now that you've given Ira to her parents?"

"Tired," I joke.

Mommy gives me a look. She won't drop the conversation without a genuine answer.

"I'm glad I did it. Glad enough that I'd seriously consider doing it again. The actual birth part sucked, but it was over fast and all those endorphins pretty much make it hard to remember just how much it sucked." I shrug.

"And everything else?" She gestures toward my body. I know she means the way the pregnancy changed my body. Changes that I dreaded and hated when they manifested. Changes I can now safely hide away with a binder, mostly.

I give the question a moment of consideration, even though I've had plenty of time to process every minute change. I knew it would be worth the reward, but seeing Jared with his daughter was even better than I imagined it would be. Much as I hated being pregnant, I'd do everything again in a heartbeat to give Jared the family of his dreams.

"I'm okay. Might need some time to kind of reclaim my body, but like, totally worth it to see Jar and Logan all glowing with new parenthood. They love her, Mommy. He loves her the way he loved me and he's going to give her the best life. The best family. And we'll get to be part of that without having to give up the things I love about not being a parent. It's the best of both worlds."

Mommy squeezes my thigh. "I'm proud of you, pup. You did a good thing."

"Yeah? I'm a good thing; want to do me?" I tease.

Mommy swats my arm. "You're seriously horny six hours after squeezing out a kid?"

I shrug unapologetically. "I'm always horny. Benefits of not relying on PIV sex, I can happily get off without using the sore bits."

"Uh, huh? Even though the doctor said to wait at least six weeks? And according to what you said about everything aching when we were leaving, it sounded like everything below the belt is currently a sore bit."

I pout. "Yeah, but six weeks sounds like an eternity."

"We'll see how you're doing after you've gotten some rest, pup. But if you push too hard too soon I won't hesitate to strap you into chastity for your own good until the doctor clears you for sex. You got me?"

"Yeah. I've got you." I smile at her. "And you've got me. Thanks for taking care of me back there."

I always understood that in theory, but after the past months, I know beyond all doubt that together, we can handle anything. Mommy will always be my rock of stability. The one who makes it safe to take any leap I set my heart on. And I'll always be the brightness in her days that brings her joy and makes her step out of her safe routines.

"I will always take care of you, pup." Mommy ruffles my hair, her words echoing my thoughts. I wish I could climb into her lap and kiss her all over, but the console is in the way. Besides, she's right that for all my bravado, I really am sore. So I content myself with squeezing her hand while we drive home. I'll have plenty of time to ease into reclaiming my post-pregnancy body. There's no rush.

EPILOGUE

Kylee

I get home from dinner and an indie film festival with a friend to find Q playing in the den with baby Ira. The two of them are making ridiculous engine sounds. Ira is propped against a pillow, sitting upright. Q has an entire fleet of chunky light up cars that sing little songs, and is driving them around for the kid's amusement.

I watch as they crash two cars into each other, eliciting a squeal of delight and a string of baby babble from our nibling. Ira notices me before Q. Her bright eyes, so much like Q and Jared's, dart to me and she points and babbles until Q rolls onto their back to look at me.

"Hi, Mommy." They wave up at me from the floor. "How was your thing?"

"Great, we ended up watching a different screening than I'd planned, but I'm glad we did. They had a few animated short films and there was one stop-motion film that—you don't want to hear my film analysis, do you?"

"I enjoy listening to anything you want to talk about, Ky." Quent gazes up at me with so much love in their eyes I don't doubt they mean it. Even if the subject bores them to tears.

"Well, I told you it was a queer film festival, right? So, before the main showing, they had an animated medley of short films. There were a couple of stop-motion ones I think you'd have liked.

Baby Godzilla coming out as a girl and then destroying the city with her supportive dad."

"Really? I might have actually enjoyed that one. Can we look it up online later?"

"Sure. There was another one that made me think of you too. Super short, only about ten seconds, but the program said it won some awards. It was just a simple clip of a paper doll transitioning, but it was really cool. Powerful in its simplicity, in a way. And something about the style being almost childlike leant it a sort of innocence and poignancy." I don't quite know what exactly made it stand out, but it did.

Quent is grinning at me like they really want to hear what I have to say. They listen with rapt attention, just because they know I care about it. God, I love them. "It was nice to see something so relatable to our experiences getting positive recognition."

"Nice. I'm glad you had fun."

"I did. And then we grabbed dinner to discuss all the nuances that would make your eyes glaze over."

"You can talk about your movies as much as you want, Mommy. Also, yummy, how was the food?" Q asks.

"Delicious as ever. I brought you home a to-go order." I hold up the bag of cheese smothered fries for my pup. Q scrambles to their feet and hugs me around the neck with one arm while relieving me of their food with the other hand.

"My hero!" They kiss my cheek.

"I see how it is," I tease them. "I get a lazy wave, but the minute there's cheese involved, you can't wait to get your grubby paws on it?"

"Well, for starters, if there weren't tiny little eyes here, I'd be on all fours showing my appreciation at your feet. And second, everyone knows fries aren't as good if they get all cold and soggy," Q points out as they step away from me to rummage through the bag. I know exactly how they'd show their appreciation, if we were currently kid-free.

The mental image of my pup licking every inch of my thigh highs to show their devotion has me curling my toes in said boots. Too bad it will have to wait until we aren't babysitting for Jared and Logan. There are definite benefits to niblings over being the parents.

Our niece is usually over here at least one night a week, nominally for the guys to have date nights. But also because my pup loves to spoil our nibling. I'm pretty fond of her too. Okay, I might spoil her worse than Q does. The fleet of light up cars might be entirely my doing, in fact.

The goober has spent entire weekends with her aunty and stork. Quent still isn't sold on having kids of our own, but I don't think it will take much convincing for them to give Ira a sibling some day. And I think this time, we'll have a better system in place to stay connected through all the changes the pregnancy will bring.

With Ira in our lives to nurture and care for, I don't feel the need to raise kids of our own as much as I did while Quent was pregnant. In my head, handing her over to Jared and Logan meant cutting the tie connecting us to her. And that couldn't be further from the truth. Ira is family and she always will be. Still, as much as we both dote on her, we're equally content to send her home with her dads at the end of a visit and return to being us.

Quent glances over at Ira, who has grabbed one of the big cars in both fists and is industriously slobbering all over the toy.

"Hey, munchkin, that's not really a chewing toy," Quent says mildly. Ira stops to favor Quent with a gummy grin, then goes back to stuffing the toy into her mouth.

"I'll watch the slobber monster while you eat." I swoop in to offer Ira a teething toy from the blanket next to her instead of the car. Mostly because batteries and moisture make me nervous, even though I got her cars designed for babies.

Q grabs a TV tray to set out their food without leaving the room. The sounds my pup makes while eating their favorite treat are downright pornographic. At first, I steadfastly ignore the noises and focus on playing cars with Ira. I sing along with the prerecorded songs, and Ira joins in with tuneless baby babble.

When I can't take any more, I glance over to give Q a warning look about teasing Mommy. Their mischievous grin tells me they know exactly what they're doing to me with all the moaning and finger licking slurps. Yep, Ira's daddies can get here anytime. I need to get my pup alone ASAP.

"Are you being a big tease on purpose, Quentin?" I ask in a sing-song that makes Ira giggle. I tickle the baby's belly, and she giggles harder before clapping both hands over mine and trying to lever my hand into her mouth. That makes me wonder if she might be getting ready to teeth again.

"Maybe." Quent draws out the word.

"You are aware of what happens to puppies who play naughty games with Mommy, right?" I ask, freeing my hand and spider-creeping it along Ira's tummy until she grabs it again.

"We win?" Q cocks their head at me.

I snort. "That depends entirely on your definition of winning, my love."

"Well, lucky for me, I consider anytime I get to play with you a win, Mommy." Quent flashes me their sweetest smile, but the innocent look can't fool me. I know them too well.

"We'll see how long you stand by that statement later

tonight."

"Yes, Mommy. I can't wait." Quent curls their tongue around a fry that's dripping with cheese, as if to emphasize their point. Car headlights shine through the den window before I can decide how I want to reply. Jared and Logan must have just pulled into our driveway. Q's phone beeps with a new text message, confirming my suspicions.

"Looks like your daddies are here, little one," I tell Ira, who is once again trying to cram a toy car into her mouth.

Q texts a quick reply, then sets aside their food. They gather up Ira's favorite paci and blanket, bundling them up with the baby's diaper bag. I extract the car from her grip again and toss it into the toy bin we keep in here for her. Ira reaches for the toy, lower lip trembling on the verge of tears. To forestall a tantrum over the toy, I stand and hurriedly lift Ira off the ground, hefting her into the air to make her laugh. Ira makes a face between a smile and a pouty lip.

"Aw, poor little Ira, is that a boo lip?" Q takes the baby from me and pulls silly faces at her. "Is Aunty Ky a big meany who takes away your yummy trucks?"

Ira babbles her agreement. She pats Q's cheek.

Q nods along consolingly. "I know. She takes away my toys sometimes too. It's not fair, is it? Your stork will get you lots more tasty trucks for next time, okay?"

They walk toward the entryway, murmuring promises for next time. I trail along after them with Ira's diaper bag. Jared and Logan meet us at the door. Tonight the hand off is quick since we all have work in the morning and the guys still have bedtime to deal with when they get home. Perks of having a nibling; we can just hand her back at the end of the evening instead of dealing with a crying baby at three in the morning. I love the little goober to pieces though.

Q gives a quick rundown on how they spent the evening with our niece. Jared comments that Ira's in different clothing than they dropped her off wearing, and checks to be sure the soiled outfit is in her bag. Quent launches into an animated explanation about how dinner went that has me making a mental note to check the kitchen for any lingering traces of strained peas.

We exchange hugs all around and then it's just Q and I. They breathe a sigh of relief and flash me a coy grin. "Alone at last. Babies are exhausting. Let's not get one of our own."

"Deal, so long as we get to continue borrowing Jar's for all the fun parts."

"Fair." Quent nods sagely. "I can't wait until she's big enough for games and movies and taking to arcades and stuff."

"Soon." I smile at the thought of my pup bouncing around a theme park with our niece. Or the two of them sharing popcorn as they gaze wide-eyed at the latest dog movie on the big screen at a theater. I'm looking forward to those days. Ice cream dates and kissing skinned knees better when Ira's learning to ride her bike and everything the future holds for her.

But I'm also looking forward to having Q worship my boots right here in the entryway, with no one to walk in on us. Being as loud as we want in bed and in the playroom. And having my pup scamper along at my feet whenever we want without having to worry about explaining things to little eyes. And sleeping through the night naked in each other's arms without interruptions.

Q catches my eye and sinks gracefully to their knees as soon as the engine noises from Jared's car fade from hearing. "I believe you wanted a demonstration of how I show my appreciation?"

"Show me," I agree, hiding the tingle of excitement their words and actions send racing along my spine. I lean back against the wall, arms crossed under my chest in a facade of indifference. Bonus points because the pose eases some of the ache from wearing a pushup bra for hours while I was out on the town. Dressing up is fun and all, but I can't wait to undress now that I'm home with my puppy.

Q slinks across the floor to me on all fours, their sinewy movements erasing all thoughts of discomfort. They're so effortlessly sexy as they bow down at my feet, knees folded under them, ass up, face down, fingers stretched toward me, awaiting permission to touch.

I nudge the toe of my boot against their chin. "Go on, lick."

Q wiggles their ass. I wish I had one of their tail plugs handy so they could wag it for me. I'll just have to imagine that part of the experience as they lavish attention on my shiny new boots. They start with suckling licks at the toes, then progress to long strokes along the arches and up my ankles.

The material is thick enough over my feet that I only notice the vague pressure of their mouth on me. I press the sole of the other boot on Q's cheek when they move too fast, slowing them down. I want to savor their adoration, not rush through it. Q whimpers at the light pressure.

"Take your time," I chide them before lifting my foot away. Q resumes their efforts, at a more sedate pace.

I savor the rasp of their tongue over leather, loud in the stillness of our entryway. When they reach the supple thinner leather over my ankles, the heat and pressure of their mouth translates through the material. I'm not sure why, but something about having my pup's mouth on my boots is empowering in a way nothing else can compare to.

This is only one of the many ways Q likes to debase themself for me. One of many forms my dominance takes. There's just something unyieldingly feminine and in control about this act for me.

Maybe it's the treasured memory of my first true taste of gender euphoria. The day I *finally* overcame a lifetime of fear to try on my first article of clothing ordered from the women's section of a store. The first thing that was mine and not borrowed in secret or hidden in shame.

I can still remember cramming my foot into my two-sizes too small dress shoes before I found online shops that carry my size. The giddy euphoria that bubbled up in my chest at the sight of my feet wearing something unabashedly pretty and girly. It was a pair of over-the-top gaudy bejeweled boots. That was my first time getting to feel unapologetically pretty as an adult on my own. Wearing those boots in my first adult apartment was when I could truly begin to envision a future I could live with.

Q on their knees, worshiping my boots with their tongue, affirms that sense of strength combined with femininity. It's an indescribable rush to have my pup so wholeheartedly believe that I have the power to guide, not just my future, but theirs too. Their tongue lovingly caresses my boots because they love me, they trust me. They adore every inch of me in much the same way that I cherish every inch of them.

I stop them before they get to the bottoms of my boots. For tonight, I've already gotten what I need from this. I lean down to grip Q's chin and lift their mouth to mine. Q opens for me, letting me guide them in a scorching kiss. Our tongues tangle and they whimper helplessly into my mouth. My needy, horny puppy.

"Bed, now, get yourself ready for Mommy." I snap my fingers. Q blinks dazedly up at me before slurping a wet puppy kiss across my lips and cheek. Then they bolt for the stairs on all fours. I follow them at a more sedate pace, detouring through the den to put away what little remains of Q's dinner.

By the time I get up to our bedroom, Q is naked in our bed, fingering themself. They've got an open bottle of lube and our girthiest dildo laid out next to them. The pretty tableau makes their desires clear.

"Ambitious, much?" I tease as I remove my clothing, starting with unclasping the uncomfortable bra. Much better. Q's eyes track the bounce of my boobs and they lick their lips. My eyes go to their bare chest.

The A-cup they filled out during their pregnancy is mostly gone now that their hormones are back to their usual baseline. They haven't expressed any lingering discomfort with the remaining hint of a swell where they used to be flat.

I could tell when they were okay with it by the way they started putting my hands on their pecs again. They cried as we made love that night, with no part of them off-limits to me. After months of that area being a no-go zone, even post-birth, it was emotional for both of us.

"Want you." Quent runs a hand along their body.

"I want you too." Eager to join them, I strip naked, pick up the dildo, and move to stand between Quent's spread thighs.

"Touch me, Mommy," they plead, eyes big and round as they gaze up at me.

I tease the toy over their groin, letting the head play over their slick folds without putting it where they want it.

"You seem to be doing a fine job of touching yourself." I sweep my eyes over their exposed flesh. From the glistening lube between their legs, up their belly that now bears the faint tracery of stretch marks, to the perfect pink buds of their nipples.

My gaze tracks up to the hollow of their throat where my collar marks them as mine. Further still to the beloved face that I want to spend the rest of my life gazing into every morning when I wake. I lean over them to hook a finger through the heart-shaped ring in their collar and urge them up for a kiss.

They arch into me, humping against the dildo I've got pressed against them. "Fuck me, Mommy."

"Such a horny little bitch. You need to get bred again, pup?"

"Yes, Mommy. Make me yours." Quent nods urgently. They grab my hand and push it onto their chest. I drop the toy, pinning it in place between us with my hips.

I squeeze a double palmful of Quent's chest, just past the point of pain, making Quent gasp and moan. It does something to me to reclaim this part of them. They're all mine again as I play with their chest, rubbing a thumb over their nipple.

We both made sacrifices to bring Ira into our family, but I don't think either of us has an ounce of regret over the experience. It was exactly the right choice for us. I know Q agrees. They wriggle under me, hips rolling in an effort to get me to slide the dildo inside of them.

"Ask me for what you want."

"I want Mommy to fuck me with my toy. Please?" Q arches.

"You want your big fat dildo shoved so far inside you that you can taste silicone, puppy?"

"Yes," Quent whines and bucks their hips into me, rubbing the toy against both of us.

I pinch one of their nipples and take my other hand off of them to guide the toy inside their body. Quent arches to meet it, writhing up off the bed. Just for that, I hold it where it is, just inside them, not sinking all the way in until I've gathered both their wrists in my other hand.

I pin their arms to the bed above their head. The position makes it harder for them to find the leverage to move under me and I ease the toy all the way inside of them with my free hand.

"Are you going to be good for me?" I tease.

Quent nods, stilling under me.

"That's my good puppy. You'll wait with this inside you for as long as I tell you to, won't you?" I wiggle the toy's base in emphasis. Quent's stomach tightens with the effort of holding still.

"Yes." Quent lets out a keening moan, but they don't move. I reward them with a gentle thrust of the toy. "Yes, Mommy. Right there, yes. Want you."

"Right here?" I ask, rubbing the head of the toy into them at just the right angle.

Quent fights against my hold on their wrists and bucks into the toy. I love driving them wild, knowing that I have this kind of power over them. The power to make them squirm, beg, and cry for me. Their body is my instrument to play, and I know just how to coax beautiful music from every inch of them.

"Yeah. Yes. Please." They struggle.

"Uh-uh. Stay." I lean over them, sealing our lips in a kiss as I slowly fuck the toy all the way into them.

I maintain the slow, steady pace until they stop wriggling. Their body eventually goes all loose and pliant under me, their legs falling open a tiny fraction more as I work them with the toy. I kiss them with all the passion and love we share.

I don't let Quent come for a long time. Not until they're begging with tears streaming down their cheeks. The need for release has coiled so tight inside them that the orgasm seems to shudder and roll through them for an eternity. When it ends, they curl into me with murmured words of love, seeking my mouth with theirs.

I'm still horny, but I could just let the urge pass me by for tonight. It's been a long day and while I wouldn't turn down an orgasm, I don't need one. Our lazy post-orgasmic kisses keep my arousal on a low boil. Quent is right where they belong, pressed against me, naked and slick. I rub against them, lazy tribbing that stimulates us both; it doesn't have to lead anywhere.

"Can I return the favor, Ky?" Quent pulls away from my mouth to ask.

Their use of my name makes it clear they're not asking permission to service me as my pup or sub. They're asking for consent to make love to me as my partner. It's not a distinction we bother with often, but in this case it means they want to give me pleasure without my telling them what to do. I nod. They fumble with the bottle of lube from earlier, coating their fingers and holding them up for me to see what they're offering.

"Yes," I agree, pressing our lips back together.

Quent hooks their legs around my thighs, pressing us together more firmly. They kiss me as they work slick fingers over my clit, stroking me with practiced movements. I rock into them, seeking more stimulation. Their lips trail along my throat, down to the furrow between my breasts, then over them, until they're mouthing at my nipple.

They continue circling my clit with insistent strokes of their fingers, trying to coax the orgasm out of me. I grind into their touch, our hips meeting, moving together as one. Quent moans and switches to my other nipple. Their free hand massages away the brief chill of air on my moistened areola when they switch sides. And, oh, that sweet suction zings through me, melding with the other sensations coursing through me. The pleasure builds to a towering crescendo, stoked by knowing it's my Quent taking me here, helping me soar in much the same way I make them fly.

"Come for me, Ky," they murmur. As they speak the words, their warm breath gusts over my suddenly cool nipple, now free of their hot mouth. The jolting contrast coupled with their words and their fingers on my clit, bearing down with just the right pressure, sends me toppling into bliss. I cling to them as I come undone.

Afterward, as I catch my breath, Quent's the one to get us both cleaned up for once. I sigh and shift to grant them access when they swab away the lube from both our bodies with a washcloth. They take the used toy into the washroom for cleaning, then tuck us both under the covers to sleep.

It's nice. Nothing I'd want all the time. That isn't what either of us wants, but every so often, it's nice to have this. Q taking care of me with the same doting care I usually shower on them.

"Mommy?" Q asks.

"Hmm?" I hum agreeably.

"I like making you come," they say, all sweet innocence.

"Mhm." I let sleep creep up on me, only half-paying attention to their words. My eyes drift shut. They're so warm next to me.

"Can we do that again soon?"

"Mhm."

"Cool. Including the part with cheese fries for dinner? I've still got a backlog from all the treats I missed out on for Ira."

"Hm," I grumble, my sleepy lassitude fading.

"Hm means yes, right?"

"Don't push your luck, pup." I crack open an eye to regard them.

They wriggle closer to me.

"Wouldn't dream of it." Q squirms into my arms. They kiss my face with swiping laps of their tongue until I push their face into my neck and wipe away the wetness with the back of my hand.

"Enough, pup, I'm sleepy."

"'Kay. Night, Mommy."

"Night, puppy." I stroke their back to help them settle.

With my hands on them, they subside into the steady, even breathing of sleep before long, and I soon follow them. I'll always follow wherever they lead. Q's wildest ideas have always worked out for us in the past and I can't imagine a future without them and their schemes. Whether or not that includes carrying a little sibling for Ira.

My worries that surrogacy would be too much for my puppy to handle proved unfounded the first time around. Sure, we had our bumps, but we made it through stronger than ever.

I've long since learned better than to underestimate their strength and determination. Not just their tenacity, but their endless capacity to bring joy into my life, repaying every bit of my nurturing care in sweetness and light. I don't think I'll ever stop falling in love with my pup, day after day, as we build our life together; no matter where our path leads, I know we'll be walking it side-by-side.

***

Thank you for reading! If you enjoyed Kylee and Q's story please leave a review to help other readers find them. For more kinky adventures, be sure to grab the next book in the series, Niko, Ethan, and Clark's story, Stud Muffin: www.amzn.com/B0B51XVMGX or catch up on the entire series at: https://www.amazon.com/dp/B09D627KGK

And for all the latest news on my writing, be sure to sign up for my newsletter: https://landing.mailerlite.com/webforms/landing/i2w6l7

ACKNOWLEDGMENTS

First, thanks to everyone who is reading this, you're the reason I get to continue writing the books I love about queer people getting their happy endings. To me, this is a story about the power of love and the inestimable importance of personal autonomy and I hope you found reading it as cathartic as I found writing it.

Telling Quent and Kylee's story was a passion project for me, and I love that I got to tell this super queer little story that has a special place in my heart. Several people helped me make the story stronger. Thank you to Amy Bellows, Kat McIntyre and Isaiah Roby for your invaluable input. This story is so much better for all your suggestions and encouragement.

ABOUT THE AUTHOR

Alex Silver (he/them) grew up mostly in Northern Maine and is now living in Canada with one spouse, two kids, and a lovebird. Alex is a trans guy who started writing fiction as a child and never stopped. Although there were detours through assisting on a farm and being a pharmacist along the way.

Visit me online at:
http://alexsilverauthor.wordpress.com/

Browse my entire book catalog at:
https://www.amazon.com/Alex-Silver/e/B07NPBW615

Join my Facebook group at:
https://www.facebook.com/groups/alexsalcove

Follow me on BookBub at:
https://www.bookbub.com/profile/alex-silver

Follow me on Twitter:
https://twitter.com/asilverauthor

Sign up for my newsletter for a free short story at: https://landing.mailerlite.com/webforms/landing/i2w6l7

And as always, consider leaving a review on Amazon or Goodreads if you enjoyed this book, reviews are of vital importance to independent authors, thanks!

OTHER WORKS BY ALEX SILVER

Summer of Adventures

Kinky Contemporary Romance

Dungeon Master (M/M)
Knotty Boy (M/M)
Service Call (M/M)
Picture Perfect (M/M)
Puppy Love (F/X)
Stud Muffin (M/M/M)

Table Topped

Contemporary Romance

Roll for Initiative (M/M) Book 1
Charisma Check (M/M) Book 2
Saving Throw (M/X) Book 3
Plus One Bonus (M/X) Book 4
Dump Stat (F/F) Book 5
Party of Three (M/M/X) Book 6

Shift Work

Omegaverse MPreg Romance

Papa Bear (M/X)
Squirrel Trouble (M/M) (expanded edition)
Trash Panda (M/M)

Hauntastic Haunts

M/M Paranormal Romance

Dan's Hauntastic Haunts Investigates:
Goodman Dairy (*Book 1*)
Hawk Lake (*Book 2*)

Ivarsson School (*Book 3*)
Joliet Asylum (*Book 4*)

Free download links to the shorts are available in my FB
group: https://www.facebook.com/groups/alexsalcove
Drew's Haunted Hangout (*A Hauntastic Haunts Short Story 1*)
Rafael's Haunted Halloween (*A Hauntastic Haunts Short Story 2*)
Lee's Haunted Holiday (*A Hauntastic Haunts Short Story 3*)

Psions of SPIRE
Urban Fantasy

Shelter (M/M) Novella 0.5
Bright Spark (MMMM) Book 1
Bold Move (MMMM) Novella 1.5
Keen Sense (M/M) Book 2
Weak Link (M/M) Novella 2.5
Quick Fire (M/X) Book 3
Clear Sight (M/M) Book 4
New Look (M/M) Novella 4.5

A SPIREverse daddy kink standalone
New Ground (M/M/X)

Shared Universe Series
Super U - Superhero Romance
Super U: Rising Storm (M/X)

Final Days - Zombie Romance
The Willows (M/M GNC)

Anthologies
Listen: The Sound of Fear
Haunt (M/M trans gothic horror)

ALEX SILVER

Fix the World
Upgrade (gay trans cyberpunk)

SUMMER OF ADVENTURES
CHARACTER GUIDE

Martin: Owner of Adventures, MC in Dungeon Master who discovers a kinky boy in the cafe where he's forced to work when his office gets flooded.

Bobby: A barista who first appears in my contemporary series, Table Topped, and finds love with a regular at the cafe where he works. Martin sweeps him off his feet with a whole new world of kink after a misunderstanding about just what sort of dungeon Martin runs draws them together in Dungeon Master.

Monty: One of Connor's closest friends. Tate's best friend. A pudgy boy with ADHD who discovers that his best friend's brother is his perfect Daddy in Knotty Boy.

Luke: Tate's step-brother and Monty's Daddy. He specializes in ropes and suspension bondage and gives workshops on the topic. He and Tate are also business partners. Realizes his brother's best friend is the perfect boy for him in Knotty Boy.

Tate: One of Connor's closest friends. A plumber who owns his own business along with his step-brother, Luke. He is dyslexic and into age play/ABDL. Finds his Daddy after a chance encounter leads to more in Service Call.

Rory: Tate's Daddy. A trans man who moves to Vancouver for his career as a voice actor and rediscovers his kinks as Tate's Daddy. Finds love after a one-night stand in Service Call.

Connor: Quent's best friend. A shy, pierced, Jewish, trans boy looking for his perfect caregiver who can also be his partner. Finds love when his kinky friend with benefits grants all his wishes in Picture Perfect.

Jackson: A kink photographer who offers Connor a kinky friends with benefits relationship the turns into so much more in Picture Perfect.

Quent: Also goes by Q. A fun loving nonbinary pup who uses they/them pronouns. Connor's best friend. They are in a long-term relationship with their Mommy, Kylee. The pair has an ethically nonmonogamous relationship that is open for sex and kink, but closed romantically. Quent and Kylee struggle to deepen their relationship when Quent offers to be a surrogate for their brother in Puppy Love.

Kylee: Quent's Mommy. She is a trans woman who is a motherly figure to all of Quent's little friends, particularly Monty, Tate, and Connor. Her story is told in Puppy Love.

Harry: A contractor who is kink positive. Harry met Quent when he helped with renovating Quent and Kylee's home playroom. He is Connor's friend group's DM for their regular D&D sessions. He also handles the renovations at Adventures for Martin.

Clark: A pup handler who appears in multiple books along with his partner. Niko is his pup and husband. They have an open relationship. His story is coming soon in Stud Muffin.

Niko/Nicholas: Clark's pup. One of the friends pup Q enjoys playing with. He is married to his handler, Clark and dating his boyfriend, Ethan. His story is coming soon in Stud Muffin.

Ethan: Nicholas's boyfriend who sometimes plays with Clark and Niko together. His story is coming soon in Stud Muffin.

Hope: Angel's Domme and partner. They have a teenage daughter, Bethany.

Angel: Hope's sub and one of Luke's go-to rope models for demonstrations and workshops. They are married to Hope and Bethany's parent. The pair appears in several books as members at Adventures.